NEW YORK REVIEW BOOKS
CLASSICS

SKELETONS IN THE CLOSET

JEAN-PATRICK MANCHETTE (1942–1995) was a genre-redefining French crime novelist, screenwriter, critic, and translator. Born in Marseilles to a family of relatively modest means, Manchette grew up in a southwestern suburb of Paris, where he began writing at an early age. While a student of English literature at the Sorbonne, he contributed articles to the newspaper *La Voie communiste*. In 1961 he married, and with his wife, Mélissa, began translating American crime fiction—he would go on to translate the works of such writers as Donald Westlake, Ross Thomas, and Margaret Millar, often for Gallimard's Série Noire. Throughout the 1960s Manchette supported himself with various jobs, writing television scripts, screenplays, young-adult books, and film novelizations. In 1971 he published his first novel, a collaboration with Jean-Pierre Bastid, and embarked on his literary career in earnest, producing ten works over the course of the next two decades and establishing a new genre of French novel, the *néo-polar* (distinguished from the traditional detective novel, or *polar*, by its political engagement and social radicalism). During the 1980s, Manchette published a translation of Alan Moore's *Watchmen* graphic novel for a *bande-dessinée* publishing house co-founded by his son, Doug Headline. In addition to *Fatale*, *The Mad and the Bad*, *Ivory Pearl*, *Nada*, and *No Room at the Morgue* (all available from NYRB Classics), Manchette's novels *Three to Kill* and *The Prone Gunman*, as well as Jacques Tardi's graphic-novel adaptations of them (titled *West Coast Blues* and

Like a Sniper Lining Up His Shot, respectively), are available in English.

ALYSON WATERS is a translator of some two dozen books from the French, including the work of Louis Aragon, René Belletto, Eric Chevillard, and Albert Cossery. For NYRB Classics, she has written the introduction to Cossery's *Proud Beggars*, and has translated Emmanuel Bove's *Henri Duchemin and His Shadows*, Jean-Patrick Manchette's *No Room at the Morgue*, and Jean Giono's *A King Alone*.

SKELETONS IN THE CLOSET

JEAN-PATRICK MANCHETTE

Translated from the French by
ALYSON WATERS

NEW YORK REVIEW BOOKS

New York

THIS IS A NEW YORK REVIEW BOOK
PUBLISHED BY THE NEW YORK REVIEW OF BOOKS
207 East 32nd Street, New York, NY 10016
www.nyrb.com

First published as a New York Review Books Classic in 2023.
Published in the French language as *Que d'os!*

Library of Congress Cataloging-in-Publication Data
Names: Manchette, Jean-Patrick, 1942–1995, author. | Waters, Alyson, 1955–
    translator.
Title: Skeletons in the closet / by Jean-Patrick Manchette; translated by
    Alyson Waters.
Other titles: Que d'os! English
Description: New York: New York Review Books, [2023] | Series: New York
    Review Books classics
Identifiers: LCCN 2023000777 (print) | LCCN 2023000778 (ebook) |
    ISBN 9781681377605 (paperback) | ISBN 9781681377612 (ebook)
Subjects: LCGFT: Novels.
Classification: LCC PQ2673.A452 Q413 2023 (print) | LCC PQ2673.A452
    (ebook) | DDC 843/.914—dc23/eng/20230127
LC record available at https://lccn.loc.gov/2023000777
LC ebook record available at https://lccn.loc.gov/2023000778

ISBN 978-1-68137-760-5
Available as an electronic book; ISBN 978-1-68137-761-2

Printed in the United States of America on acid-free paper.
10 9 8 7 6 5 4 3 2 1

SKELETONS IN THE CLOSET

I

THE PHONE rang. I smiled apologetically and picked it up.

"Tarpon Agency," I said fawningly.

"Is that you, Tarpon? Coccioli here. Officer Coccioli. Remember me?"

"Yes."

"I'm sending you a client. Surprised?"

"A bit."

"Well, it's true. I thought of you because it's an odd case. An old lady."

"I know." (I looked at the old lady sitting across from me on the other side of the desk and smiled a second time, winking to let her know I wouldn't be long. In exchange, she blinked and smiled. Her smile was twitchy. Clearly she wasn't comfortable seated in my leatherette armchair; she would've preferred a harder chair. She was the sort to sit on the edge of her seat, lean forward, set her elbows on the desktop, and shove her pointy snout forward to blather on and on and on. Postal workers and insurance-company employees must've wasted a ton of their time listening to her explain, discuss, and ask for clarifications; that's the kind she was. She sat uncomfortably on her pointy bottom in the leatherette armchair because she couldn't manage to stay perched on the edge; she kept sliding toward the back. And she wasn't what I'd call an old lady, but still.)

"Oh, she's there already?" said Coccioli on the other end of the line.

"Yes."

"Fine. Listen, I'll call you back and explain everything, but, in a nutshell, I've sent her to you because she's a friend of the family, see, and she said she absolutely wanted to meet with what she called a private detective. I had to send her somewhere or else she would've gone to some crook who might've ripped her off. Be a pal and listen to her story, but whatever you do, don't tell her that what she's asking is impossible. Okay? Hey, Tarpon, you still there?"

"Yes."

"Okay. Don't tell her it's impossible, all right?"

"I'll see," I said. "It'll depend on my assessment of the situation."

"What! What?" cried the officer, shocked. "What assessment?"

"Mine. My understanding. You know, all that stuff—understanding, assessment, free will. You must've heard of those."

"Oh, great. Be witty. Perfect timing," barked Coccioli. "Listen, tell her you'll take on her case, you'll need a couple of weeks, and that your rate is twenty grand a week. We could've really sent you up the creek last year, Tarpon old man, what with that Sergent business, so you owe us something. And if you rip her off for more than forty grand, I guarantee you'll have me on your back. She's broke, for God's sake. Have a little heart, Tarpon, fuck!"

"I haven't said no," I remarked. "I'll see. Call me back in about an hour."

"You don't have to do anything, Tarpon. In fact, nothing *can* be done. Take the forty grand, sit tight, and in a couple of weeks you can tell her that you got nowhere, end of story. Agreed?"

I sighed and hung up. I placed my elbows on the desk, crossed my hands under my chin, and looked at the lady affably, pleasantly, and discerningly. She was wearing a dress made of Liberty cotton that must have been from the days of Liberty ships, with a lilac-colored background (the dress, that is), and a black wool jacket, black stockings, black lace-up shoes with square three-centimeter heels, and a black lacquered straw hat. She reminded me of my mother, who lives in the Allier region, but my mother is seventy; this old lady was at least ten years younger, which is why she wasn't what I'd call an old lady. Yet you could see she'd entered her golden years, maybe only a few days ago, and probably in one fell swoop: gray hair and a waxy complexion, no makeup or jewelry, just a big fake pearl on her hatpin. She had a large black purse from which she'd taken out a twenty-two by twenty-eight centimeter brown paper envelope.

The envelope contained handwritten pages and different-sized photos—amateur snapshots—mostly of the old lady's daughter at various ages between birth and thirty-six. I know because the old lady took the photos from the envelope and set them on the desk, making a running commentary as she did so. From time to time she would consult her notes.

As far as I was concerned, the profusion of photos wasn't necessary. One of the most recent ones would have sufficed, but the old lady was determined to give me a detailed bio of her daughter, which was harmless I suppose, and she wanted it to be illustrated.

In other words, she told me the story she wanted to. I said the police and the gendarmes were much better equipped than I was to do the work she was requesting. Unable to put her pointy elbows on my desk, she grabbed the edge of it with both hands, thumbs underneath, to explain that of course she'd already been to the police, but they kept telling her to be patient and that there was nothing new to report. Even an inspector she knew personally, that is, a friend of her sister's, Inspector Coccioli, who was the one who suggested she come to me, had told her there were no new leads.

"Normally I charge at least two hundred and fifty francs a day plus expenses." (I lied. I charge more. Well, whenever I can.) "So you see, it's expensive, with no guaranteed results."

"I've calculated what I can pay. One thousand new francs," said the old lady.

Looking at her, you had the feeling that was her entire savings.

"Here's what I propose," I said, spontaneously and with passion. "For four hundred francs I'll take your case for, let's say, two weeks, in my free time."

"Do you have a lot of free time?"

"In truth, yes, quite a bit," I said.

In truth, I'd hardly worked for five weeks. Before that I'd done a bit as a watchman in a warehouse where there'd been some attempted arson, and at the moment I was trying to figure out if one of the six employees in a pharmacy was stealing from the till like the pharmacist suspected.

The old lady thought for a moment and then said okay. She gave me a check. We shook hands, I walked her to the door, we shook hands again, and she left.

I looked at my watch. Almost six in the evening on Saturday. It was Bébert's day. Bébert, otherwise known as Albert Pérez, twenty-nine years old, pharmaceutical assistant, employed for the past three years by Jude's Apothecary.

I put on my black scarf, then slipped my gray three-quarter-length coat over my brown three-piece suit. Coccioli hadn't called me back. Too bad. I had my calls forwarded to the answering service, grabbed my briefcase, and went downstairs. In the apartment building entranceways and cafés, and on the sidewalks, the hookers were, predictably, on the job: leather shorts, tennis skirts, and forced smiles. On the roadway cars poured out of Porte Saint-Martin like a roll of armadillos and then stopped short, shoulder to shoulder, vibrating in a cloud of blue gas. I decided not to take my Citroën 2CV in case Bébert pulled the same stunt on me as last week. I took the Métro at Strasbourg-Saint-Denis and read most of *France-Soir, Le Monde*, and *Le Parisien libéré* over the shoulders of my neighbors, then came back aboveground at Saint-Germain-des-Prés. According to *France-Soir*, the present situation was disastrous. *Le Monde* said it was cause for serious reservations. And according to *Le Parisien*, the French were demanding more austerity. I walked to the bottom of boulevard Raspail with a stop at the chess bookshop on boulevard Saint-Germain, where I bought the November issue of *British Chess Magazine*. I slipped it into my inside coat pocket.

At the end of boulevard Raspail, I picked up the rental car I'd reserved, a big Fiat. They showed me where the gearshift was and I took off. It was 6:45 p.m. I hung a right at Sèvres-Babylone, and then another right through the neighborhood of ministries and expensive old apartment buildings, passed in front of the late Onassis's property, and got back onto boulevard Saint-Germain. With all the traffic, my fifteen minutes was up. At 7:00 p.m. sharp, I double-parked among all the other double-parked cars on the left side of boulevard Saint-Germain, across from Jude's Apothecary, which was closing.

At 7:01, Albert Pérez walked out the door at the same time as a couple of female pharmaceutical assistants, and behind them Mr. Jude closed the grate and locked up from the inside. In the meantime, our man Bébert—a tall, thin guy with very dark hair, blue eyes, and muttonchops, an American cigarette in his yap, and wearing a long sheepskin jacket—arrived at the pedestrian entrance of the Saint-Germain-des-Prés parking lot, which swallowed him up.

When his Simca Rallye 2 drove out of the lot and headed in the same direction as last Saturday, I was already on the rue de Rennes. Much farther along, after the Montparnasse train station, across from Bigeard's butcher shop in the vicinity of boulevard Pasteur, he finally passed me. Half an hour later, he crossed the Pont de Saint-Cloud, with me a hundred meters behind him. The previous week, I'd followed him in my poky 2CV, but I'd lost him even before the tunnel exit. Typical. This time, I tailed him until he got off the Rouen highway and beyond, along a hilly state road, all the way to Dieppe. He didn't respect the speed limits at all, and twice I thought I'd lost him, but in the end I hadn't.

It was just after ten when we got to Dieppe, but our man Pérez went straight into one of the few hotels open during the off season, among all those that line the promenade facing the sea. Like he was a regular there. I didn't see why I shouldn't do the same. I waited for five minutes after he went into the place with his little canvas suitcase and then I went in with my briefcase. As the fat man with no tie at reception was handing me a key, and while I was wondering where I could find a place to sit and read casually while watching to see if Bébert would head out again, guess what? Old Bébert came straight back down.

"Good evening, Mr. Pérez," the receptionist cried cheerfully, collecting the key that Bébert was tendering him between thumb and index finger with an arm movement that was graceful and showy, like an entertainer in an American comedy. And Bébert went out. I couldn't, in all decency, do the same.

When the fat man walked up the stairs in front of me huffing and puffing to show me the room, which was cold and damp with beige wallpaper decorated with hunting scenes in neo-prostitute style, when I gave him a one-franc piece as a tip, and when he walked back out through my door, and when I shut it behind him, I ran to open the window but it was much too late to catch a glimpse of Mr. Pérez, Albert, no doubt out of sight already for a good while, either because he'd gone down one of the alleyways or because he'd walked onto the huge esplanade-promenade that separates the seafront from the sea, and where the lighting, in this off-season month, was somewhat lacking.

I didn't see Albert Pérez but, to the left at the end of the esplanade, right on the shore, below the cliff where the Dieppe Castle Museum sits with its paintings, maritime trophies, and carved ivory collection, I saw a sort of giant kiosk with multicolored lights that, no doubt about it, was the Dieppe Casino.

Before going in, I decided to take a shower and treat myself to some mussels and fries and a beer near the port. I figured Albert must be in the casino and I doubted he'd split before midnight.

Just after midnight, I crossed the promenade, the vast esplanade intersected by a maze of roads for cars, dotted with streetlamps. Not a soul in sight. You could hear the roar of the waves in the dark. A cold north wind carried water and salt across the city, stinging my ears. I walked around a miniature golf course and into the casino. The movie theater inside, where the latest Charles Bronson film was playing, had been closed for a while, but over by the gambling and the band there were people, even a crowd, in sharp contrast to the desolate Siberian character of the esplanade.

Albert Pérez was at the chemin de fer table. He had a considerable pile of chips in front of him. As I was watching, he won another fifteen thousand francs from the banker, a fortyish man with a Roman nose and rectangular eyeglasses. The banker had just said *"J'en donne"* with a rather strong accent, American I think, and put down a four and two threes with a moan of displeasure. Fifteen thousand francs also went to a little guy with a shaved head at the end of the table. Then someone else was the banker. I didn't understand how the game was going because I don't know how to play chemin de fer. All I know is that Pérez was betting very unevenly, sometimes huge sums and sometimes peanuts, and that he lost peanuts and won shitloads. At this rate, he'd be there a while.

I went to have a drink in the nightclub where four Black guys wearing dashikis were playing music and the sons of fish traders and the daughters of store owners were dancing, while their parents were shooting the breeze at huge tables set up at the back of the room. I slowly sipped a scotch and water, thinking about what the old lady had told me earlier that day.

Her daughter, Philippine Pigot, had disappeared a month ago. She was born during the war, a war baby and a bastard ("Her father died in the war, she didn't know him," Madame Pigot had told me), single, and blind since birth. Blond, five foot seven, well built, and quite pretty judging by her picture. She was athletic. She seemed to be doing quite well in life despite her infirmity. Swimming, horseback riding (accompanied), and even dancing ("She isn't trying to do anything artistic, it's just a sport, you know?"). She had a job that paid okay as a braille typist at a certain Stanislas Baudrillart Foundation, which was dedicated to the social advancement of the blind. She lived with her mother in their house in Mantes-la-Jolie and took the train morning and evening five days a week to go to and from her job in Paris.

In August, she'd spent her vacation in Greece at a holiday resort. She'd gone back to work in early September, and in late September she'd disappeared. One Tuesday, she'd left for work like every morning, but she never got there and hadn't been seen since. The police did their usual search. In the absence of clues, not much turned up.

"Did she have friends or acquaintances in Paris?" I asked her mother. "I suppose all that has already been verified, but—"

"No friends, no. Her office mates."

"But other than that? A ... a man maybe?"

"No."

"Sorry, but can you really be so sure about that?"

"I'm her mother, Mr. Tarpon."

"Of course, Mrs. Pigot, but still."

"She didn't have the time, sir. She did everything on schedule. She never ... dawdled or anything like that. She was never late."

Which proved absolutely nothing, obviously. The pool, dance classes, horseback riding, vacation, her commute—all of those are full of men, and women as well, and there are always holes in the schedules of the living, but I dropped the subject.

I asked a lot of other questions, not all of them pertinent, and what came out of all that is that nothing came out that attracted attention. I was just stuck doing the routine verifications that the police had already done. I was almost ready to follow Coccioli's advice and do nothing at all.

"In the days immediately preceding her disappearance, did anything unusual happen?" I asked. "Did she come home a little agitated, or abnormally calm, or, I don't know, anything? Did she receive any phone calls?"

"No."

"You're sure?"

"Absolutely."

Mrs. Pigot's answers flew out of her mouth like tennis balls. Those answer-balls throw you off balance because they aren't answers; they simply mean that your interlocutors have decided to give you a particular answer and not another one. And if that's what they've decided, it's usually because they've formed an opinion that they want to stick to, either because they have enough information to have formed a precise and correct opinion or because they don't. And sometimes, too, it's because your interlocutor is lying to you. That's what I was saying to myself as I sipped my scotch and water.

2

I WENT back to Paris on Sunday afternoon. Albert Pérez had won a stack of money on Saturday night. At 10:00 a.m., as I was wolfing down a sticky croissant with a muddy cup of coffee, the lab assistant came racing down the hotel stairs, his face cheerless and his chin unshaven, and he left immediately, canvas suitcase in hand. I hadn't had the time to follow him. A little later I hit the road for Paris, stopping on the way for a modest feast at Mr. Jude's expense.

In Paris, I passed Porte de Clignancourt, and on rue Championnet, where Albert Pérez lives, I saw his parked Simca. I went to return the Fiat to the rental agency and then took the Métro home.

My answering service gave me the list of calls that had come in since the previous day. Coccioli was first, asking for me to call him back, but he didn't leave a number for me to do so. Then someone who hadn't left a message or a name. Then Charlotte Malrakis, inviting me to a party at her place the following Saturday and asking me to call back to confirm. Then once again someone who left neither message nor name and who'd called back twice that morning. I thanked the answering-service employee and took back my phone line.

I began by calling Mr. Jude at his secondary residence and gave him a brief summary of my weekend. He started boiling with rage at the other end of the line and calling Albert Pérez all sorts of awful names.

"I want that little shit to go to prison," he screamed. "I want him to wish he were dead. What should I do? Call the police?"

"Well," I sighed, "if he'd lost last night, I would've said yes. A guy who steals money and who loses when he gambles lives in fear, right? All the cops need to do is shake him up a bit, and he'll crack."

"Exactly!" (He sounded both happy and nasty.)

"But he won last night. He's in heaven. We have no proof. There's one chance in two that he won't crack. Actually, I'm not sure he's our guy." (Unintentionally I made a disgusting noise with my saliva.) "On the other hand, if we wait until he loses again, he won't be in any shape to reimburse you, if indeed he is our guy."

"I don't give a fuck about the money!" Jude cried. "Take another week and get me some proof. What I want is for him to be punished. Get it?"

"Got it."

"Figure it out. Do what Maurice Thorez did."

"Excuse me?"

"Don't be afraid to stick your dick in the riffraff," he declared, extremely pleased with himself, and he burst out laughing.

I sighed. "I'll call you back at the end of the week," I said.

"Just remember." (He'd grown nasty again.) "I want my thief in prison. I want him to eat shit."

"I'll remember."

We hung up. I was depressed. Before I became a private investigator, I was a gendarme. Not the good kind who warns you not to speed, finds runaway kids, and sorts out the tragedies of alcoholics, nope. I was in the mobile unit—that is, I spent most of my time waiting in police vans, not allowed to get out, with a gnawing need to pee. Every now and then we'd break up rowdy groups of protesting workers. I killed a guy. And I quit. (Since then, my colleagues got a new model of van, with built-in latrines. But even with the built-in latrines, I wouldn't have been at ease in the gendarmerie anymore.)

If I became a private investigator afterward, I think it was partly because I wanted to do Good, like I was taught in catechism and in the Boy Scouts. And where am I now? With the down-and-out. I track down poor dumb bums to stop them from stealing from well-heeled guys like Mr. Jude, while drug traffickers sit on the National Assembly and everywhere else. And what can I do about it?

In other words, I was depressed.

The phone rang. I picked it up.

"Tarpon Agency."

"Eugène Tarpon?"

"Who's calling?"

"You'll see. Will you be home in the next hour? I'm coming over."

"It's Sunday," I remarked.

"I'm eager to see you."

"Fine. I'll wait for you." (After all, I didn't have anything do to on my Sunday. What was left of it, that is.)

The man—his tone was curt, childish, not very refined, authoritarian, and antipathetic—hung up. I went to unpack my bag, that is, I opened my briefcase and put away my pajamas and toothbrush. I picked up *British Chess Magazine* and returned to my office. I removed my miniature chessboard from a drawer and took up my *Harrap's* dictionary. I started to re-create a game from two or three months ago (while Philippine Pigot was in Greece) between Lhamsuren Myagmarsuren and Tudev Ujtumen in Ulaanbaatar during the Mongolian Spartakiad. I hope that's clear. In any case, Ujtumen won in twenty-eight moves. In order to understand the commentary, I had to keep looking up words in *Harrap's*. What's great about chess is it makes me learn English, and you can defend yourself better in life if you have a second language.

When I'd finished replaying the game, as I was putting the pieces back in place, someone rang the doorbell. I placed the dictionary and chessboard back in the drawer and went to open the door.

He came in pretty much as I'd expected, his chin raised high, his arms at his sides, a half-turn of his torso and wham, shoulder first: everything was supposed to get out of the way of the real tough guy. But I'd only opened my door about forty degrees and after that, as if by chance, my foot blocked it. So that he banged his shoulders against the doorframe and stupidly bumped the side of his face on the door.

"You okay?" I asked.

He snorted. "Tarpon?"

"You the one who called a while ago without giving your name?"

He started walking in immediately so that our foreheads almost slammed into each other because I didn't budge. He made a valiant attempt to pull himself together.

"Charles Pradier," he said. "It's about Philippine Pigot. Can I come in now?"

I nodded and stepped to the side. We walked through the anteroom, which also happens to be my bedroom, with its blue sofa bed, pedestal table, and magazine rack, and went to sit down in the other room, which is my office. (I also have a kitchen, and that's all. The toilets are on the landing, and there are public baths on rue des Écluses-Saint-Martin, if you care to know.)

Charles Pradier was a tall, skinny, brown-haired guy with blue eyes. His hair was thick and he had sideburns. He looked a little like Albert Pérez. He was wearing a beige loden coat over a silk suit. There was some odd trick in the weave of his suit; objectively, it was a very dark gray, almost black, yet it had purple reflections. At night under certain lights, it must have been practically phosphorescent. It was all exquisitely tasteful. With that, he was wearing a very wide tie with designs resembling butterfly wings and a pearl gray shirt. A gold tie clasp was fixed on his tie at the base of his sternum, and he also had a gold Masonic signet ring. His English shoes were mahogany colored. He took a blond-tobacco cigarette out of a gold case, inserted it in a Dunhill cigarette holder rimmed with silver, and lit it with a Laurimette lighter advertising Mazda lamps. I waited patiently.

"Well?" I said finally. "What about Philippine Pigot?"

"She didn't disappear. She split from home."

"Who said she disappeared?"

"What?" he said, leaning his head toward me. "Oh, yeah! I see! You wanna know how I knew that the old lady had come to see you. The police, old man."

"Really. The police know."

"Whadda you mean, the police know?" (Again he pushed his head forward, his neck taut.) "No! Not at all! But my buddy wrote to them. Philippine Pigot split with my buddy."

"Your buddy?"

"His name matters little," said Pradier bookishly. "I don't know the . . . how can I put this . . . psychological details, all right? But the fact of the matter is that they were seeing each other, my buddy and her. And so, my buddy went to set up shop abroad, because he's a businessman. And so, the girl decided to follow him because she loves him. He loves her too. It's a love story, see? Now if you're wondering why Philippine didn't explain the situation to her old lady, don't ask me. I'm not in their shoes. It's a generation-gap thing, see?"

I sort of saw.

"Do you know Philippine?"

"Of course!" (He glanced at me suspiciously.) "I mean, not all that well."

"Is she a blond or a redhead?" I asked.

Ten seconds went by, he sat there with his kisser open, and he looked lost, hateful, then clever in succession.

"Hah! What a joke!" he exclaimed. "She's a brunette!" He was glowing at the thought of having escaped a subtle trap.

"What's your buddy's name? Where is he?"

"Oh, sorry, I can't tell you that."

"You expect me to take you at your word?"

"Of course not!" (He was glowing ever brighter. He dug around the inside pocket of his coat that he'd unbuttoned but not removed.) "I've got a message! A letter from Philippine." (He took out an ordinary envelope on which MON-SIEUR E. TARPON had been typed. The envelope was bulging. He held it out to me.)

"She'd probably be better off writing to her mother," I remarked as I opened the envelope. "You'd probably be better off going to see her mother."

"Honestly, Tarpon, did you ever try to justify yourself to a mother? She'd jump down my throat and alert the neighbors. I'd find myself with the police on my ass. They're in love!" shouted Pradier ardently. "They want to be left the fuck alone! Understandable, no?"

I let out a groan devoid of any particular meaning. In the envelope was a single large sheet of light brown paper as thick as a manila folder, smooth on one side and fluffy on the other. On the bottom of the smooth side, there was a big signature made with a fat-tipped felt marker. The signature took up almost the entire width of the paper, something like fifteen or eighteen centimeters. Most of the sheet above the signature, if you looked closely, was covered with little bumps, as if the paper had been put in backward in a typewriter without a ribbon and as if someone had typed lots of little dots at random, very forcefully, on the back of the sheet.

"What on earth is this?" I asked sensibly.

"Why, it's braille, of course," Pradier replied, even more sensibly. "The poor kid is blind."

"So it's typed on some kind of machine then?"

"I have no idea. I'm not blind. They gave it to me like that."

"Yeah, well, old man," I said, "as far as I'm concerned, a typed message with just a handwritten signature..." (The signature was very clear: PHILIPPINE.) "No, I don't buy it. I should take things into my own hands and call the cops. And I just might do it."

"Before you do," said Pradier, "you might want to call Officer Coccioli. You'd see we brought a message to the police that they found completely satisfactory. If you call the cops, that'll just cause both of us problems and complications. It's pointless."

"Can you give me your address?"

"I'd rather not."

"Fine," I said. "I'd rather call the cops anyway."

He became visibly agitated in his chair. "Listen, Tarpon—"

Just then the phone rang. I answered. Pradier looked at his watch, one of those very practical and inexpensive things that you have to push on with the other hand so that the numbers light up.

"Monsieur Tarpon?"

"Speaking." (I thought I recognized the voice.)

"It's Madame Pigot. Marthe Pigot. I have to talk to you right away." (She was screaming into the phone, but I don't think Pradier could hear. Just to be safe I pressed the phone tightly against my ear.)

"Do you want me to come to you?" I asked.

"No, not at my place or at yours. Meet me at the Saint-Lazare train station in the waiting area at seven thirty tonight."

"I can be there earlier, you know." (I couldn't say more seeing as Pradier was a mere meter from me and was looking at me placidly through the smoke of his second cigarette.)

"No, 7:30, Saint-Lazare station."

"Okay."

She hung up. I put the handset down and pressed on the hook with my index finger. On the third try, I got the dial tone.

"Excuse me a second," I said to Pradier, trying to hold his attention while attempting to feel my way to dialing the emergency number.

"Oh, no. I said no cops," he stated rather calmly as he got up.

I opened the drawer where I keep my dictionary and my chessboard. I have a gun, but it was at the bottom of a metal filing cabinet, underneath my clean sheets.

"If you take one step toward the door," I threatened nervously, "I'll kill you."

He just laughed in my face, the boor, and turned his back to me and walked toward the door, hands in pockets. Over the phone I suddenly heard the dulcet direct-distance dial tone, which just goes to show that when you try to dial the cops without looking, you get a wrong number. I plunked the handset down on the hook and rushed after Pradier. I caught up to him in the vestibule just as he was opening the front door. He turned on his heels, whipped his hands out of his pockets, and sent his right fist straight into my jaw. I ducked under the fist and bashed the lower half of his sternum with my head. This hurt my head and he fell backward, his mouth open, his arms flailing. He crashed against the kitchen door with a dull noise. I turned around to go get my pistol in the other room and right then someone opened my front door behind me and hit me on the head with an anvil or something.

I fell on all fours. I headed for the other room in this position. My thoughts were in a muddle, but I was still aiming to get my gun.

Someone hit me again, this time in my lower back and that really hurt, whereas I no longer felt anything in my head. I fell on my side.

"Get up, you little idiot!" said the guy who'd anvilled me, but he was talking to Pradier who was having trouble recovering on the floor by the kitchen door.

In the end, the anvil guy, whom I could barely see—I only managed to make out a shape in a raincoat or a trench coat—grabbed Pradier by the neck, pulled him to a seated position, and towed him toward the exit.

"Ooh-ooh," Pradier groaned. "Let me, ooh-ooh, stomp on his, ooh-ooh, balls, ooh." (In all likelihood Pradier was talking about my organs, but the other guy dragged him outside and Pradier was too weak and groggy to impose his viewpoint. They shut the door behind them.)

It took me about three or four minutes to feel well enough to stand up. It was too late to run after them and my windows look out on the courtyard, not the street. Good going, Tarpon. You really nailed that one.

I had a small cut on my scalp and blood had run down the back of my head onto my neck. I stripped to the waist. My jacket was clean, but my shirt collar was stained. I put my shirt to soak in the sink. Then I put some rubbing alcohol on my head. The rest of me was in fairly good shape. I had a pretty good-sized lump on my head and a pink spot on my lower back. It'd all really hurt tomorrow morning.

At last I put on another shirt and went back to the phone. I called Madame Pigot in Mantes-la-Jolie but no one answered. It was almost 7:00 p.m. I put my tie, my jacket, and my coat back on and headed out to the Saint-Lazare station.

Night had fallen. The sale of flesh in my neighborhood was going strong. The Métro was fairly crowded with workers in their Sunday best coming home from a snack at Auntie Jeanne's, slapping their overwrought kids around; conscripts out on the town; British school kids yapping in unison; tense Arabs; and homeless beggars.

I got to the Saint-Lazare station at a quarter after. When I saw the posters in front of the Saint-Lazare Pasquier movie theater, I remembered that Charlotte Malrakis was a motorcycle stunt woman in the movie playing there, which reminded me that I'd forgotten to call her back.

I hung out a bit in the station waiting room. Other people were waiting too. Others were arriving. Others were passing through.

At 7:34, Madame Pigot appeared, hurriedly, almost running toward the middle of the waiting room. She turned around and saw me. I waved to her and walked toward her. She ran toward me and just then her head exploded.

3

THIS WAS some bullet. Not a vulgar dumdum bullet, not one clumsily carved with an X to break up on impact and do as much damage as four. No, it was a carefully made bullet, so that it had a regular, circular concavity at its tip—a bullet, traveling at about the speed of sound, say three hundred meters per second, that pushes a ball of compressed air in front of it. It's sort of like being hit by a billiard ball traveling at the speed of sound. The person firing at you doesn't even need very good aim. If a projectile like this strikes you in the arm, that'll do it: the impact alone will kill you.

Madame Pigot was struck behind the ear. She fell as if she were flinging herself facedown. Three or four seconds went by before anyone realized exactly what had happened. Besides me and the shooter, that is. I hadn't heard the gun go off—the guy must've had a silencer and there was a lot of noise in the waiting room, and quite a few people. I had no idea where the shot had come from; I stood still watching people scramble. Then a woman began to scream when she realized what had spattered all over her. Other people yelled and shouted, giving out information and advice. (Careful. There's been an assassination attempt. Call someone. Don't touch her, she's wounded. It's a grenade. Run!) There was a bit of a panic, and then a crowd formed.

Meanwhile, I'd managed to get a vague idea of the angle

of fire and strode quickly toward the other side of the waiting room, staring at the people all rushing in the same direction. Since I didn't see anyone whom it seemed wise to ask, "Excuse me, sir, but did you just shoot down a woman over there?," I went back the way I'd come. There was now a huge throng around the corpse, along with four uniformed policemen who seemed to be arguing with the crowd. All of a sudden, you could hear a racket of sirens outside. Six other uniformed officers appeared and sprinted inside.

Previously, as I was nearing the crowd, I'd flattened something small with my heel. I stopped and looked down at the ground covered in cigarette butts and used tickets, and I picked up the shell casing I'd stepped on. It was empty and crushed but you could still make out SUPER-X and 45 AUTO on it.

"Move aside, please," an officer said to me.

The cops were in the middle of closing off that part of the waiting room and chasing out everyone who wasn't supposed to be there.

"But I need to make a spontaneous declaration."

"Wait here, we'll take your name."

I had to hold him back by his sleeve.

"I saw everything. I was supposed to meet the woman who was killed. And I think I've got the shell casing here. I don't see what else it could be. My prints are on it. Sorry."

"Your prints?" said the cop, taking the casing from me. "Oh, shit, yeah," he said, tossing the casing from one hand to the other as if it were a hot potato. "Chief!" he yelled. "Chief!"

A little later, after I'd identified the dead woman and myself, and offered a few other details, and after more officers arrived—plainclothes this time—they led me away.

I waited until 9:30 p.m. in a hallway, guarded more or less by an okay cop who even offered to sell me a sandwich, but I turned it down because the way Madame Pigot died had spoiled my appetite; plus, I had a headache.

From 9:30 p.m. until 2:45 a.m., I gave my statement to an inspector named Chauffard and two officers who took turns questioning me. Chauffard wasn't a bad guy. Chubby, with a toothbrush mustache, he worked quite diligently and didn't act like he was a hero in a Western or Inspector Maigret. The officers, on the other hand, were rather tough, obviously with his blessing. This whole bunch grilled me for quite a while because I'm a private investigator and my profession is full of crooks, con men, and gangsters. I told them everything I knew and repeated it forty or fifty times until they were satisfied.

At about 10:15 p.m., after my first statements, we went to my place in a cop car to pick up the message in braille signed "Philippine." Then we drove back to the station, where one of the deputies disappeared with the letter and came back without it. Later, when Chauffard told me I could leave and that I could expect to be summoned back to the station at any time, I asked him what the letter said.

"Nothing important."

"That letter belongs to me," I objected. "Don't you have a transcription of it?"

He sighed into his mustache and picked up a piece of paper someone had brought him earlier. I don't know how he managed to locate it right away in the mound of papers covering his desk. He did have big eyes, though.

"'Dear sir,'" he read. "'I've learned that my mother has hired you to find me. It's completely pointless. I left of my own accord to join my fiancé, who has a job abroad. I don't want to see my mother, at least not at the moment. So you're wasting your time and my mother's wasting her money. I'd be grateful if you could share this message with her.'" (Chauffard looked up with his big sad eyes.) "That's it," he said. "And 'Philippine Pigot' is typed above the handwritten signature. Okay?"

"Now that her mother is dead," I said, "maybe Philippine will show up."

"I should hope so!"

"Me too." I sighed.

"Go home and leave me the hell alone," Chauffard commanded.

Which I did, in reverse order.

Once I got home, I rubbed liniment into my aching lower back and ate the last of a half an unripe Camembert with some day-old bread in the kitchen. Then I opened the sofa bed and climbed in, groaning because of my lower back. I was afraid the events of the evening would keep me from sleeping, but they didn't.

On Monday at 2:15 in the afternoon, after having slept like a log, I was awakened by Officer Coccioli pounding on my door. I let him in.

"Just a friendly visit," he said, tossing *France-Soir* and several envelopes onto my unmade bed. "It's my day off. I was in the neighborhood, so . . ." He gestured toward the pile on the bed. "I brought up your mail."

I made us some instant coffee. While the water was boiling, I shaved and got dressed, then came back with two cups and we sat down in my office where I'd brought in *France-Soir* and the rest of my mail.

For a guy who was making a friendly visit on his day off, Coccioli seemed tense. He's a tall guy with very straight brown hair combed back from his face, olive skin, dark eyes, a large hooknose, full lips, and slightly bucktoothed. He has an easy smile; when he smiles, he squints and it looks as if he's in pain. At the moment, he wasn't smiling at all, and he was constantly running a hand through his hair. He was also nibbling on his lower lip that already had bite marks on it.

I flipped through *France-Soir*. Madame Pigot's murder was on the front page, but in very small letters, just a headline that told you to look inside, where there were two columns that took up a third of the page, with no illustrations. "Shooting Victim," said the subtitle, "Had Meeting with Private Detective." I glanced through the article. A certain Inspector Madrier was in charge of the investigation. I looked up from the paper.

"I was interviewed by Inspector Chauffard last night," I stated. "And here it says—"

"He was taken off the case. I know Madrier."

"Oh."

We stared stonily at each other. I hadn't asked anything of Coccioli. He was tapping his left palm with his right fist.

"Antonin Madrier," he repeated after a moment. "I know him. I worked with him in Marseille four years ago."

"Oh."

"In the financial division of the regional police. We were disbanded."

"Oh?"

"Reassigned all over the place. We got promoted. Especially Madrier."

"Oh," I said again.

I was glancing at my mail. I'd fanned out the envelopes on my desk. There was an offer to subscribe to a weekly paper, a telephone bill, a bank statement, and a letter. The letter had been mailed at midnight last night in Mantes-la-Jolie. You could tell from the postmark.

"Is Coccioli a Corsican name or an Italian name?" I asked.

"It's Italian, but I'm Corsican."

"A guy came to see me yesterday afternoon to tell me that everything was fine, that Philippine Pigot had left, that she hadn't 'disappeared.' And he told me to call you if I didn't believe him. Basically he said that the police had received a message from either Philippine or her fiancé, I don't really remember which, and that the police were totally fine with everything."

"I don't see how a simple message could make everything 'fine' when someone's disappeared."

"Neither do I."

"All I know is that Antonin Madrier is in charge. Of the girl's disappearance I mean. Your instant coffee is disgusting. You put in three times too much." (Nonetheless he drained his cup and put it back down with a grimace that looked like a smile.) "I know what the guy who came to see you told you. I looked at the file before Chauffard was taken off the investigation. There's nothing you might have forgotten to say last night?"

"What do you care? You're not the one in charge of the case."

"No, I'm not," said Coccioli. "Madrier is." (And he smiled as if someone were poking his stomach with a hard object.)

I picked up the envelope from Mantes and opened it on my lap. The only thing inside was a photograph.

It was an amateur snapshot of a couple smiling next to a crib in a garden. A young Marthe Pigot was wearing a blouse under a jacket with padded shoulders and a skirt that came to her mid-calves. Her hair was in a bun in the back and all curly in the front. The man, whose legs were hidden by the crib, was wearing a dark-colored uniform shirt and an Alpine Hunter beret. The woman was younger than thirty; the man was probably ten years older. The beret was overexposed.

On the back of the picture, a few lines had been scribbled in pencil; the writing was large and hurried: "Sunday 6:15— Tarpon if I don't make it to the meeting—he will have made me disappear too—It was Philippine's father—She recognized him six weeks ago—I didn't believe it—FANCH TANGUY." This name was in capital letters, underlined three times with quick strokes; then the signature: "Marthe Pigot."

"Since you don't have a client anymore, and the police have the matter in hand," said Coccioli, "I suppose you'll let it drop."

I turned the picture over in my hands twice more, and then I raised my eyes toward the officer who was looking at me with a falsely guileless expression—it was really more like the expression of someone who sticks his nose where it doesn't belong. I tossed the envelope and the photo on my desk and nodded toward them for Coccioli to take a look. He looked and read and looked again.

"All we need in this fucking mess," he said calmly, "is a guy from Brittany."

4

THE DECEASED Marthe Pigot had lived with Philippine in a rented apartment in downtown Mantes-la-Jolie. I had the address. I left the 2CV some three hundred meters away, after having passed in front of the place slowly, trying to see if there were any cops hanging around.

In the hallway, a mailbox told me what floor the apartment was on. I went up on foot because there was no elevator. The building was old, solid, cozyish, and a little run-down. The stairway carpet was threadbare and the paint was peeling below the tall narrow windows. The landing floor squeaked.

I thought I might try to have the concierge show me around the Pigot residence. I have some old papers from when I was a gendarme, and ordinary citizens rarely know for certain that a gendarme never works in plainclothes. Still, I tried the latch with a plastic card case and the door opened. I went in, closing the door behind me.

The apartment was almost square, with a central hallway. To the right lay the kitchen, bathroom, and one bedroom; to the left, another bedroom and the living room. The decor was gloomy and the furniture bulky, mostly dark brown, Henri II style. The armchairs and the heavy drapes were bronze green. Cheerful. All of it was outdated.

The phone was in the hallway. I walked in front of it then stopped, turned around, picked up the handset, and unscrewed the mouthpiece. Inside was a tiny microphone shaped like an aspirin. I left it there, screwed back the mouthpiece, and hung up the handset.

In Philippine's bedroom, a braille typewriter sat atop a pedestal table with twisted legs. There was also a horrible doll about fifty centimeters tall, outfitted like a Gypsy in a red dress with a comb in her hair, sitting on the cozy-corner bed. I didn't dawdle. When you're searching a place, you have to have particular things in mind or else you need to go through everything, which takes hours. I went into the other bedroom and opened the closet. Five or six rather elegant dresses, two equally elegant suits, stylish shoes, etc. No hats.

In the bathroom, I found the black lacquered straw hat with its long hatpin and the big fake pearl, with the church-mouse dress and the black stockings. All of it had been tossed on the floor in a corner between the radiator and the basket of dirty laundry. When Marthe Pigot had come to our meeting at the Saint-Lazare station where she'd been gunned down, she'd been wearing a fake-fur coat.

I left the apartment. Outside it was getting dark and had started to rain. It was cold. It was truly shitty weather. I raised my coat collar and strode toward the 2CV.

"In a hurry, Tarpon? Find what you were looking for?" Charles Pradier asked me as he appeared out of nowhere on my left and fell in step with me.

I glanced to my right, toward the road. Someone was walking one step behind me and he pushed me gently forward by my elbow.

"Don't be a fool. We just want to talk to you. Let's walk to your car."

I didn't answer. We walked to my car and got in, me at

the steering wheel, Pradier next to me, and the other guy in the backseat.

"Don't turn around," he said, as I was about to do so to stare at him. He stopped my head from turning by grabbing a fistful of my hair. I grimaced because he was pulling on my scalp where it had been injured the day before. "Answer me," he ordered. "Did you find what you were looking for?"

We were there, in my car, in the cold, with harried people passing by on the sidewalk less than a foot away, and cars stalling on the road in the heavy traffic. We were totally isolated in what felt like a casket and Pradier patted me down quickly to make sure I wasn't armed. The windows were dripping with rain, adding halos around the neon signs of the stores and traffic lights.

"What were you looking for?" Anvil Man asked again, since I wasn't answering.

"Are you by any chance Philippine's fiancé?" I ventured.

"What were you looking for, Tarpon?"

His voice was patient and calm, his elocution precise, as if French weren't his mother tongue. He was a totally different animal from Pradier, and I think he was starting to scare me.

"Nothing in particular. A clue of some kind," I said slightly grotesquely. Pradier sniggered. "Listen," I said, "when Marthe Pigot came to see me, she was dressed like a little old lady from the country. When she was killed, she was wearing a fake-fur coat and other things . . . I just wanted to see how she usually dressed."

Anvil Man let out an approving groan. "And what did you conclude?"

"Nothing. She wanted me to think she was a harmless simpleton, I suppose, when she came to see me. And maybe she wasn't harmless for everyone." (I sighed and waved my hand eloquently.)

"And what the hell do you care about that, Tarpon?"

"'Scuse me?"

"She's dead. And she's no longer your client. You don't have a client anymore. Why don't you let the police deal with the matter?"

"The lady," I declared cinegenically, "paid me for two weeks of work in advance."

Behind me Anvil Man let out a disgusted snort. "Who asked you to work on the case, Tarpon?"

"Let's say it was Fanch Tanguy," I answered.

I don't know what got into me to say that. Maybe I wanted to see their reaction. I looked Pradier straight in the eye and he didn't react in the least, but behind me I heard Anvil Man suck in air through his teeth, and then I heard a characteristic click. No doubt about it, Anvil Man had retracted the breechblock of a semiautomatic weapon.

"We'll have to talk about that somewhere else, then. Start the car." (Pradier shot him a surprised glance.)

I started the car. Anvil Man told me what direction to take. We drove out of Mantes and headed toward Meulan on Route 190.

"Slow down," Anvil Man ordered as we were nearing a protected intersection. "Now turn left." (I turned onto a torn-up local road. Pradier looked surprised again.)

Night had fallen and in the darkness a car was coming in the opposite direction with its high beams on. I raised my right hand and adjusted the rearview mirror. At the second when the other car arrived next to us and whooshed by, the inside of the car was lit and in the rearview mirror I clearly saw Anvil Man's face. He was over forty and looked Scandinavian. He was wearing a Prince of Wales hat with a narrow border pulled down. He had a shadow of a salt-and-pepper mustache and blue eyes that were staring straight at me from behind rimless glasses.

We kept on driving, but now I knew he was going to kill me in a few minutes, probably as soon as he'd found the right spot. Then the deserted road began to descend a wooded hillside.

"Slow down," said Anvil Man.

I turned ever so slightly to the right and we ran smack into a mile marker.

The 2CV hadn't been going fast, but still. I had seen it coming and had braced myself with my feet, so I went upward, my head in the soft part of the roof and my heels on the floor, but I hit my hip bones very painfully against the steering wheel. Pradier's head and shoulders had gone completely through the windshield. The Scandinavian Anvil Man, who'd been the best protected, was flung forward and his hand wound up wedged between the two front seatbacks, a hand that was armed with a Colt .45 automatic with an enormous silencer the size of a turnip.

Meanwhile, the engine block was being crushed, the hood was popping up toward the heavens, the windshield was exploding while Pradier was going through it, and all four doors burst open. The entire car was lifted about thirty centimeters off the ground then fell down on its shock absorbers with a clang.

I fell down at the same time, roaring in pain, and immediately grabbed onto Anvil Man's wrist. A shot went off with a *pow!* and a hole five or six centimeters in diameter appeared in the dashboard. I pushed down as hard as I could on the wrist, using the bar between the seats as leverage. The wrist snapped.

"Ha," said the Scandinavian. Nothing else, just "Ha!" and he bopped me on the ear with his left fist.

I tore the pistol from his broken hand, but I kept a tight hold on his wrist because I wanted us to stop hitting each other and talk like civilized folk, but he persisted in slugging me on the ear with his other fist, and then he drew his knees up under his chin and bucked. The entire front seat was torn off its base and I was half crushed between my seat and the steering wheel.

I let go of his broken wrist. The Scandinavian dived head-first out of the open door. I aimed at him over the seat but I hesitated for a second because I knew that with this gun, it wasn't possible simply to injure someone. He rolled himself up in a ball and disappeared down the slope, into the fields and the night.

I got out of the car as quickly as possible. Pradier hadn't budged since the impact: he was lying with his stomach across the hood and his legs inside. As far as I could tell in the dark, his face was bathed in blood. I walked around the car. I was doubled over from the pain in my hips and I could only move forward sideways, like a crab.

In the dry grass, maybe two hundred meters away, I thought I could distinguish a light-colored blob making a getaway. I aimed the .45 with both hands, but it was difficult, and I was trembling like a leaf. And then the light-colored blob disappeared.

I leaned on the wrecked 2CV. Sweat was dripping into my eyes. I was having trouble breathing. My breath made a plume of condensation in the air. Yet it wasn't particularly cold. I must have spiked a fever for a second. A repugnant stench of manure was coming from the dry grass. Here and there in the valley, you could see the lights of some rather big villages with people, stores, bars, music, means of payment—in a word: civilization.

After a little while a car raced down the road. It slowed as it reached the 2CV, then sped up again and disappeared. I hadn't signaled to it. I went around the wreck again and ferreted out a flashlight. My Kelton watch had broken and stopped at 7:54. I lit up Pradier's face. His throat was open, his eyes too, his tongue between his teeth. He was dead.

I suppose you could call the state I was in an altered one. In any case, I set out across the fields, still walking sideways. After a bit my muscles warmed up and I could advance more quickly. I found a main road and stuck out my thumb. A priest in a Renault 4 picked me up and dropped me off in Pontoise. From there I took the train back to Paris and from the Saint-Lazare station I got on the Métro. I went home. I turned on the light in the vestibule and closed the door. Just then someone lit a desk lamp in the other room. I pulled the .45 out of my pocket and pointed it with outstretched arm. I had to come up with a good argument to convince myself not to shoot.

"Eugène Tarpon?" said the guy sitting at my desk. "Commissioner Madrier."

I looked at him. He was a tall, wide man, not fat but massive, with the broad face of a baby pig, a small snub nose, pouty lips, light blue eyes, stringy curly hair, about forty years old. He was wearing a camel-hair coat and a pearl gray fedora tilted back.

"Kindly stop pointing that thing at me, will you? I said I'm Commissioner Madrier."

"Prove it."

He shook his head, smiling as if I were a temperamental child, and with his left hand, pulled back the side of his coat and the jacket underneath so that I could see his inside pocket. With the thumb and index finger of his right hand, he slowly drew out his wallet. He placed it on the desk and opened it. I went toward it without taking the gun off him and walked through the doorway more or less expecting to be attacked from the side, but I wasn't.

"Are you alone?" (I picked up the open wallet.)

"I like working alone. Do you believe me now?"

I lowered the Colt and gave him back his wallet. Madrier stood up, still smiling affably, and put away his wallet.

"What is that monster?"

He stretched out his left hand and took the .45 from me. He put on the safety, then tested the weight of the gun and amused himself aiming at the wall with his arm outstretched, like a real pistol lover.

"Long story," I sighed.

"The silencer throws it off completely." (He was having fun toggling the safety.)

"I think this is the weapon that killed Madame Pigot," I said.

"I see."

He pulled the trigger. The shot went off and dug a crater in the wall the size of a tangerine.

"Darn, what an asshole," he said, laughing as if he hadn't done it on purpose.

But I got the message. When, with his right hand, he pulled an MR73 revolver out of his pocket to take me down, I'd slid my hand behind the metal bookcase and toppled it onto his face.

5

THE TROUBLE with Commissioner Antonin Madrier was that he was too sure of himself. After the metal bookshelf struck him on the side of his head and he fell down on one knee, and the heavy furniture bounced on its side and crashed onto his right hand, I found myself totally unprotected for about two whole seconds. He could almost have shot me at close range with the gun in his left hand. But he didn't because he hadn't thought of it. With a cry of rage and pain, he violently tore his ravaged right hand, which was holding the MR73, out from under the bookshelf. The movement destabilized him slightly and his torso fell backward; his left leg was stretched out flat against the floor and his other leg was bent under him, his right foot under his ass.

I grabbed the .45 with both hands and kicked the commissioner in the crotch with all my might. He let out a scream and, in a frenzy, slammed me in the ribs with the side of the MR73. I stumbled over his left foot and fell on my back, banging my head against the radiator. I was holding the big automatic. I saw the commissioner's face just as he was pointing the MR73 at my stomach and I shot him.

Instinctively I aimed for his shoulder but that didn't change much; as I said, with a weapon like that…I saw Madrier get up from the floor for a fraction of a second, then fall on his back, limbs akimbo. Where his shoulder had been, it looked like Soutine's *Still Life with Dead Sheep*, and his mouth and eyes were open wide. His eyes were bloodshot—totally scarlet—from the impact. In the corner of the room two meters from the corpse, the floor and walls were spattered with blood. The whole room reeked of cordite.

I tottered to my feet, hanging on to the radiator that was burning my fingers, but I didn't feel much. I simply felt numb. My knees were trembling. I walked around the corpse. Something was dripping on my face and I put my fingers to it and then looked; it was only sweat, like before. Without thinking I picked up the MR73. I put the safety on both weapons and stuffed them in my pockets, the revolver on the right and the automatic in my inside pocked (my left outside pocket was torn and burned and sticky). I tried to think but couldn't. The only thing that came to mind was that I'd actually seen the inside of the mouth of an MR73, a dull black hole.

I left the apartment. I walked down the stairs, faster and faster. I shot past the rusted sheet-metal sign that read: PLEASE WIPE YOUR FEET, EVEN IF YOU USE AUFFRA SHOE POLISH. Once on the street, I started to run. I don't remember much about what happened next, but no doubt I took the Métro. After that, I was in a modern elevator. The automatic doors slid open. I walked down a windowless, carpeted landing paneled in plywood, past a bench. I looked at the labels next to the doorbells, the ones with names. I found what I was looking for. I rang the bell. Charlotte Malrakis opened the door after a moment.

"Holy shit!" she said with a joyful expression on her face. "If it isn't the gendarme Eugène Tarpon!"

I stayed on the doorstep rocking back and forth and looking at her. She eyeballed me and frowned. She disappeared for about twenty seconds and came back with a glass of water and threw it on my face. I nodded, blowing through my lips and spitting out a little water, and then I started to laugh. Charlotte stepped back in alarm.

"Whoa!" she said.

"It's nothing. Just ... I can think now ... Why I came here," I muttered. "But it's over. Don't be scared."

"I'm not scared," said Charlotte, intrigued. "What happened? Are you drunk?" (She looked at my left side.) "What's wrong? Shit, you're covered in blood."

"No, no," I said and stepped into the room with drops of water in my eyes and one drop on my nose, and then I fell flat on said nose.

Then it was daylight behind the blinds and I was lying snug and warm in bed. I'd just opened my eyes. I couldn't make out much in the half-light. I remembered the black hole in the mouth of the revolver, and then I remembered the rest. I sat up abruptly and felt a sharp, paralyzing pain in my side. I calmed myself so I could think. After a moment I palpated my left side. I noticed first that I was wearing only my boxers and shirt. My shirt was torn on one side. Almost the entire left side of my rib cage was extremely painful to the touch. But I had no open wounds. My hip bones, lower back, and head were also hurting.

Just then, Charlotte arrived. I was worried when I heard the door open, but I relaxed when I saw her lit from behind in the doorway because I recognized her. And she glided into the room on tiptoe.

"I'm awake," I said.

She turned on a light. She was carrying a shopping bag. Like the Scandinavian guy, she was wearing a trench coat. She also had on a pair of skinny dark blue corduroy pants and sneakers. She has a small build, a small triangular face, smooth skin, and long brown hair that falls to her shoulders. The more I think about it, the more delightfully beautiful I find her. She placed her shopping bag on the carpet.

"You okay?" she asked in a rather cool tone.

"I'm fine."

She went over to the large sliding window and raised the blinds with a long-handled crank. Daylight flooded in. It was a large studio with a kitchenette. It had a double mattress on which I was lying, lots of beanbag chairs and cushions, two walls completely covered in book and record shelves, a portable TV on the floor in the middle, and a rather monstrous quadraphonic installation with speakers as massive as dressers. All kinds of pictures were attached to the walls with thumbtacks: a portrait of Marilyn Monroe; a portrait of Clark Gable; other portraits of people I didn't know but who seemed to be movie stars from before the war, except for a skinny Black woman with a Chihuahua and a cigarette holder who seemed to be a singer or something; and a poster of the cover of *The Saturday Evening Post* from June 12, 1937, signed Norman Rockwell; and other things as well.

Charlotte came back to the middle of the room. She took some newspapers out of her bag and tossed them on the bed. Then she picked up the bag and went into the kitchenette. I saw her take a package of ground coffee from the bag. She opened it and filled an electric coffee pot. Next she crossed the studio until she reached the record player and started up the quadraphonic installation, putting the arm of the record player onto an album that was already on the turntable.

In the meantime, I'd sat up in bed wincing a little and grabbed the papers she'd tossed at me. There was *France-Soir* (this informed me the day was well advanced, since it only comes out in the afternoon) and *Le Parisien libéré*. I was on the front page of both of them with, in *Le Parisien*, my photograph. THE "CRAZY" PRIVATE DETECTIVE read the headline of *Le Parisien*. SHOOTOUT IN LES HALLES said *France-Soir*. Both of the dailies decided I was most likely the killer with a .45 who'd shot down Marthe Pigot in Saint-Lazare station and, busted by Commissioner Antonin Madrier, assassinated him with the same weapon. According to *France-Soir*, the chances that I was the killer were very strong; according to *Le Parisien*, it was certain. According to *Le Parisien*, I had "already made headlines last year on the occasion of sadistic crimes committed in the circles of leftists and sexual perverts." I folded up the papers. The quadraphonic installation was piping out high-pitched, tuneless music that was getting on my nerves. The coffee pot was spewing steam. Charlotte unplugged the pot.

"Thanks," I said.

"You're welcome. Are you in pain? I called a doctor."

"Huh?"

"Last night. A friend. It doesn't look serious. You've actually got an appointment in a little while for an X-ray, but..." (Her voice trailed off.) "You've had a terrible shock," she articulated clearly. "Probably someone shot you at close range and missed you by a hair."

"No, he hit me with the side of the revolver and it went off."

Charlotte poured coffee into two cups.

"I didn't even realize it," I said.

"You were covered in blood, Tarpon. You were soaking in it. Over thirty square centimeters of your body. I was so scared!"

"I apologize. Could you please shut off the angry cat? I'm sorry, but my head..."

She laughed.

"Still the hick, Tarpon. I wake you up to Marion Brown and you complain. Do you remember Chick Corea?" she asked as she walked toward the record player, and since I was shaking my head looking lost, she said we'd already listened to Chick Corea last year, when she'd been involved in some nasty business. While we were driving, the radio had played Chick Corea and I'd wanted to change the station. Didn't I remember? And I said no, sorry.

She stopped the music, shaking her head. She came back next to me and offered me some sugar. I pushed away the sugar bowl, shaking my head. She put some sugar in her cup. We weren't speaking anymore and she was looking at her coffee with a nasty air.

"I killed that police commissioner," I sighed. "Last night I killed Commissioner Antonin Madrier."

"I'm not asking you anything," Charlotte said.

As a result, I told her everything, absolutely everything.

We had another cup of coffee. About halfway through my story, she also poured us a little pear brandy in two tasting glasses.

She listened to me earnestly and asked an intelligent question from time to time. What I was recounting was rather horrifying, but it was almost pleasant to tell it to her.

"But the bookshelf?" she asked. "Why did you dump it on him?"

"He was about to kill me then. The .45 came in handy, see? He'd come to kill me in any event, but the .45 came in really handy. There would have been a bullet from the .45 in the wall to prove I'd opened fire on him with the automatic, and that he'd killed me in self-defense. In fact, his plan worked perfectly." (I motioned toward the papers on the bed.) "Except that he's dead," I added.

Charlotte giggled. I looked at her, confused and irritated.

"Your Commissioner Madrier is a chump."

"Ya think? And maybe I'm not up shit's creek?"

"Still," Charlotte said, "he was a real asshole. May his ashes rest in peace." (She giggled again, which only exacerbated my irritation.) "He should've shot you right off the bat. He could have made his holes in the wall after."

I stared at her with my jaw hanging open, and she was still giggling, the little bitch. She let out a sigh and went over to the record player. She flipped through her albums. Every now and then she would glare at me, or else she would giggle some more.

"What do you want me to play, old man? I don't have any accordion music. And what do you plan on doing?"

"I don't like the accordion. Can't we just spend five minutes without music?"

"Not easy," said Charlotte.

"I'll go to the police," I said. "I don't have a choice."

"You'll be toast if you do."

She went into the bathroom and came out right away with my clothes and the .45 and the MR73.

"It won't be a piece of cake, that's for sure. But I'm innocent. So there has to be another explanation. We'll talk and we'll find it."

"The fuck we will!" shouted Charlotte. (She has a potty mouth that often shocks me.) "There isn't a single cop you can trust right now. Jesus, Tarpon, this thing has ramifications for the police."

"What thing?"

She threw my clothes and the weapons on the bed and raised her arms in a fury. Her breasts are lovely.

"I don't know what thing! You're the investigator! Investigate!"

"No," I said. "You're doing very well. You're wonderfully compelling. Go ahead. Explain it to me."

She let herself fall to her knees near the bed, picked a crumpled pack of cigarettes off the floor, and lit a bent one with a match from a matchbook.

"That guy Fanch Tanguy," she said calmly, "carried off his daughter. When the girl's mother finally decided to tell you his name, she was dispatched by a killer. When you found yourself in the presence of this killer, as soon as you said the name Tanguy, he decided to shoot you. And since he missed you, Commissioner Madrier came to wait for you at your place to take you down. Madrier knew you were going home with the .45, or else the whole thing doesn't hold water. Madrier and your killer were working together. They were both following Tanguy's orders. It's obvious!" (I wanted to say something but she signaled to me to shut up and she raced on.) "And it goes above Madrier's head. There are people who took ... the first commissioner off the case. I can't remember his name."

"Chauffard."

"Yeah. They took Chauffard off the case to hand it over to Madrier. Jesus, didn't you tell me Madrier had been promoted after some sketchy deal?"

"I'm not the one who said that, it was Coccioli."

"Good old Coccioli," said Charlotte dreamily.

"And then," I said, "Coccioli didn't say anything specific, he just implied some things."

"Enough already! Madrier has been in cahoots with them since then."

"Yeah, yeah, of course," I muttered in a vain effort at irony; she was on a roll. She downed her brandy in one gulp and held her head with both hands.

"Oh my God, Tarpon! Oh my God! It all makes sense!"

"I'd love to share your optimism," I said.

"You call that optimism? Tarpon, you'd better write all that down and head straight to the newspapers." (She stood up and raced to the back of the studio. She pushed over a pile of magazines and grabbed a Hermès Baby typewriter that had been under the pile.) "Five copies!" she shouted, lowering a folding desk and practically throwing the typewriter down on it. "We'll go straight to *Libération*, straight to *Politique Hebdo*, and straight to *Le Canard enchaîné*, and we'll hold on to two copies."

"Hey, wait up there," I said. "Mind if I decide what to do?"

She looked at me. "If they're killing everyone who ever heard the name Fanch Tanguy," she said, "I'm next in line, old man."

6

I REFLECTED a moment while Charlotte was cheerfully turning over piles of paper then cursing because she couldn't find any carbon paper.

"Listen," I said at last, "let's make a deal. I'll leave here." (I got out of bed, a bit embarrassed to be in my undies, and my ribs and my hips were killing me. I grabbed my clothes and started to put them on.) "I'll leave," I repeated. "And I won't mention you and no one will ever know I saw you. In exchange, you won't write to the papers and you'll keep out of all this."

"No I won't!"

"Yes you will! You wouldn't happen to have a razor, would you?"

She walked into the bathroom ahead of me, waving her palms on each side of her face.

"It's your life insurance, for Pete's sake, Tarpon!"

"If things are the way you described them, it'll cause one of those messy scandals . . . So no way. I don't want the cops and God knows what or who else on my back for the rest of my life. Okay, I'll write a letter, but it will be addressed to a lawyer. Open only if something bad happens to me. You get the picture."

The bathroom was a disaster, with an overflowing laundry basket and bras and panties hanging from a drying rack.

Charlotte placed a Gillette razor, a tube of shaving cream, and a shaving brush on the side of the sink. She smacked each object against the porcelain and her lips were pursed. I turned on the hot water. I wet my cheeks. I slathered on some shaving cream and grabbed the brush.

"These belong to your husband?"

"Yeah."

"Last night when I got here, you threw a glass of water in my face, right? Why?"

"You looked weird."

"I wanted to fuck you."

"Huh?"

I lathered up my entire face. I looked at my face full of foam in the mirror.

"It was more or less unconscious," I said. "It's because I saw two people die a violent death in the course of a couple of hours yesterday, and because someone tried to kill me twice."

"So nice of you to think of me."

"It wasn't really thinking."

When I'd finished washing and shaving, I joined Charlotte in the other room. She was standing in front of the window, looking out. I sat down on the bed and checked my weapons. There were three cartridges in the Colt's magazine and four in the MR73's six chambers. I took the silencer off the Colt because it was easier to carry in two pieces. I put my burned, torn jacket on over my torn, stained shirt and grabbed my coat, which was even more damaged.

"Wait," said Charlotte.

She went to open the sliding door of a closet and came back with a long sheepskin jacket. I put it on. It fit perfectly.

"It's Nick's," said Charlotte.

"Thanks. I'll return it. Where is Nick?"

Charlotte shrugged. I emptied the pockets of my jacket and coat.

"Look."

I held out the photo that Marthe Pigot had sent to me. Charlotte looked at it for a long time, front and back, then returned it to me.

"What *is* that uniform?"

"It dates back to the Occupation," I said. "I think it's from the Milice." (I pocketed the photo.) "Well, thanks for everything. Bye." (She didn't answer.) "You're pissed at me, aren't you?"

"Yes."

"Listen," I said, "I have no intention of negotiating with them. It's just that I don't want to get the press involved when I don't even know... when I don't know a thing. Because that's what's called burning your bridges. I'm the son of farmers, angel. I don't burn anything."

"Get out. Fuck off."

"I can live without your respect."

I left, closing the door very softly behind me.

From the Buttes-Chaumont neighborhood where Charlotte's studio is, I took the Métro to Montparnasse, then the local train toward Versailles. I got off at Clamart and walked for some time. The town was full of construction sites and new apartment buildings; Clamart was changing. Back in the day it was a town of vegetable growers; they still hold an annual pea festival. Then the working families took a hit when the limestone quarries collapsed causing the mudslide of 1961, and they lost the little houses they'd managed to buy with every centime they'd saved. And now the old folks are dying off one by one. So the little houses are being razed to the ground and replaced by apartment buildings with glass doors where executives of every political stripe, with their briefcases and trendy rectangular eyeglasses, come to live.

There are still some neighborhoods that have a majority of private houses with small gardens on the curved streets with their uneven sidewalks. It was to just such a neighborhood that I was heading, southeast of the station, about two kilometers from the train line. I walked along the picket fences, pushed open a screened gate, and went down a gravel path until I reached a two-story cement house, two times as high as it was wide, stuck like a tooth at the edge of a vegetable garden. In the distance, you could hear construction-site machines and jackhammers. I climbed the front steps. I went in.

Haymann was in his immaculate living room, sitting in a huge worn-leather armchair, wearing wide gray flannel pants and a beige crewneck sweater, his feet in slippers. He was reading Conrad's *Nostromo*. I looked at him for a moment from the front door (I'd come in without making a sound). Then he saw me over the top of his book and stared at me, coldly and pensively. He placed his open book facedown on the side table.

"Well, well. It's not our game day, Monsieur Gendarme."

"You didn't see the papers?" (I walked into the room. Suddenly I felt a bit weary and my bruises were hurting.)

"I hardly ever read the papers since I've stopped writing for them," said Haymann. "But Coccioli brought them to me. You wanna drink?"

I dragged my hand across my stomach. "I'd rather eat, frankly."

"I've got some ham."

He stood up and went into the kitchen. I followed him. He took plates and silverware from a cupboard and placed them in my hands. I went back to the dining room and set the table on the scarred oilcloth. Haymann came in with the ham he'd taken out of the fridge, two glasses, and a liter of red wine. We sat down at the table. Haymann grabbed a travel chess set off a shelf.

"A quick game while we eat?"

I sighed. He unfolded the chessboard in front of us and had me pick a color from his closed fists; I was black. He opened by moving the king's pawn two spaces. I chose to open with the Pirc Defense.

"So, Coccioli decided to come, did he?" I asked. "Was he on the job?"

"That's not quite the impression he gave me. He wanted you to contact him."

"What did he mean, contact him? More like he wants to nab me."

Haymann shook his head and pouted.

"I don't know," he said. "I'm not sure. Did you really kill that Madrier commissioner guy?"

I nodded. He stroked his chin with a grating sound. He hadn't shaved that morning. His beard fuzz was white.

"You're really up a creek. I'm going to take your pawn."

He took one of my pawns. I shouldn't have chosen the Pirc Defense on a day like that because it demands a whole lot of attention during the first ten moves. I took the photo Marthe Pigot had mailed to me out of my pocket and held it toward Haymann. He examined it without touching it, squinting. He stood up and went to get his glasses from a dark blue metal case. He put them on and came back to stare at the photo without sitting back down, a fist placed on the table and his rear sticking out. His lower lip was drooping slightly, revealing bottom teeth yellowed with tartar; his breathing was audible.

"Do you know who this guy is?" he asked.

"A certain Fanch Tanguy by chance?"

He nodded as if we'd been talking about Tanguy just the other day.

"Fanch the Whistler. Is there a relation between the shit you're in and Fanch the Whistler?"

I explained everything to him. He nodded and I could still hear his breathing. After a minute, he sat down and drank three large glasses of red wine while still listening to my story. I didn't mention Charlotte Malrakis.

"Fanch the Whistler," Haymann repeated when I'd finished, and he sighed and smiled and his smile wasn't a pleasant one.

"I thought he might be wearing a Milice uniform in the photo. That's why I came to you. Why do you call him Fanch the Whistler?"

"Because he whistled," Haymann said. "He whistled the *Danse macabre*. You know the one I mean?" (Haymann whistled a few bars; he whistled off-key.) "Apparently, he was impressed by Fritz Lang's movie *M*. There's a homicidal maniac in that movie, I think Peter Lorre played the role, and he's always whistling the *Danse macabre*."*

"I've seen the movie. Hey—" (I interrupted myself. Haymann looked up and gazed at me, intrigued. He asked me if something was wrong.) "I'm fine," I said. "Isn't there a

---

*In the movie *M*, Peter Lorre is compulsively whistling a theme of Grieg's, not the *Danse macabre*. Haymann is mistaken, or else Tarpon is misquoting him. [author's note]

blind beggar in that movie? He recognizes the killer when he hears him whistling, right?"

"Yeah. Oh! I see where you're going!" said Haymann. "But it's not possible."

"Why?"

"Fanch the Whistler died. In '44."

"For God's sake, will you please tell me who Fanch the Whistler is!"

"I'm trying. But you keep interrupting me. Fanch the Whistler was a piece of shit. He belonged to the PNB, the Breton National Party. Hand in glove with the Krauts. To such a degree that the fascist PNB kicked him out, if you can believe it. Around '43, he turned into total scum. A bit Milice, a bit French gestapo. He was definitely connected to the French gestapo. Racketeering, extortion, spying, torture. And he would whistle while he ... while he ..."

"Take it easy, Haymann," I advised.

He leaned back in his chair, took a deep breath, and with a swipe of the back of his hand, sent the chessboard flying into the middle of the room. The pieces were everywhere. We looked at each other and I didn't say a word. Then Haymann calmed down.

"I have cousins by marriage who dealt with Fanch the Whistler." (He lit a Gitanes Maïs cigarette.) "You know how we Jews are. We lose our cool so easily."

"Okay, okay," I said. "What else can you tell me?"

"I've got files in the basement on this kind of thing. I'd have to look at them if you want details."

"That'd be good. Whenever you can. And what about Marthe Pigot? Does her name ring a bell?"

"Not at all. But she must have been a Pétain supporter if

she gave that name to her daughter. But . . . maybe Pigot is not her real name."

"And Fanch Tanguy is dead? Are you sure?"

"Fanch the Whistler was collared in '44 by a member of the Corps Francs when he was driving toward the Spanish border in a Citroën filled with money and jewelry. He was killed. I don't know the details. But let me think a second. I can find you a firsthand witness. I just have to make a phone call, okay?"

I spread my arms. I didn't know where any of that could lead, but it had to go somewhere. So I nodded. Haymann got up from the table and went to make a call on the huge telephone from the dinosaur age at the other end of the room. Then I got up from the table and picked up all the chess pieces. I heard Haymann asking to speak to a certain Captain Melis-Sanz, and then there was a short conversation in Spanish. I don't understand Spanish. Haymann hung up.

"Everything's good," he said. "We'll see our guy tonight."

"What time is it?"

"Ten thirty. You've got a watch."

"Yeah, but it's broken. Did Coccioli say anything about how I should get in touch with him?"

"Just to call him. He left a few numbers. Say, do you know a guy about forty-five years old, glasses, trench coat, a Prince of Wales hat, and his right arm in a sling?"

"Why?" I asked.

Haymann looked outside through his white cotton curtains.

"Because he's pacing in front of the house."

I closed the chessboard, took out the MR73, released the safety, and set the revolver on the table.

"He's the guy who bopped me with an anvil," I said. "If things go south, just start shooting. The chamber in front of the firing pin is empty, the next four are loaded. Be careful. The guy doesn't pull any punches."

"Hey!" said Haymann. "Wait just a second!"

But I was already in the entrance and I walked through the door, taking the .45 out of my pocket. The Scandinavian Anvil Man had stopped pacing and now he was leaning against the screened gate. He was smoking a cigarillo. He glanced over his shoulder and saw me.

"Turn around slowly and face me," I ordered.

He obeyed. His features were drawn. His right arm was supported by a long black scarf. His hand and entire forearm were in a cast that went past his elbow, up a third of the biceps, so that he hadn't been able to put his trench coat on his right side, and the sleeve hung empty.

"Don't do anything you'll regret, Mr. Tarpon," he said. "We've got Charlotte Malrakis."

7

"CHARLOTTE who?" I asked after a moment.

"May I?"

He motioned toward the inside of his trench coat. I blinked.

"Slowly, now," I said.

He gently slid a color Polaroid snapshot out of his inside pocket and held it out to me. In the photo, Charlotte was naked, tied and handcuffed to a metal chair that was bolted to a cement floor. In the field of vision, an anonymous hand was holding a copy of the day's *France-Soir*. The date was not legible but the headlines—including SHOOTOUT IN LES HALLES—were clearly recognizable so that there was no question that the photo was as fresh as fresh bread. Charlotte was a bit disheveled and she'd been crying; there were traces of mascara running down her cheeks. Still, she was trying to put on a brave face. She didn't appear to be wounded. I stared at Anvil Man.

"Slowly," he said back to me.

"Yeah, yeah," I mumbled clumsily, then added: "I've written a detailed letter to my lawyer. If you hurt that young woman, I promise you that all of France will hear about Fanch Tanguy."

He nodded. "You're complicating my life. It took me too long to find you. We're going to have to resolve this business through negotiation."

"Negotiation my ass," I said with a vulgarity that wasn't really my style. "You're going to release Charlotte Malrakis." (He smiled mockingly.) "Fine. What else do you have to offer?"

"You and the old guy in the house there" (he lifted his chin toward Haymann's place) "are going to come with me. Now. I don't have the authority to argue the point. I'm taking you somewhere where people will be able to discuss things with you. You'd be better off putting away your weapon. The neighbors will wind up noticing something and we don't want to attract any attention, now do we?"

I didn't respond. I tried to think. From his pocket, the Scandinavian Anvil Man delicately lifted out a tuft of brown hair and sort of dusted off my nose with it.

"I yanked it out," he said, showing me the roots of the tuft. "If the negotiations haven't begun by midnight, my colleagues have been instructed to saw off one of Charlotte Malrakis's fingers. Until then, minor injuries to her will become more and more unavoidable as time goes by."

I smacked him upside the head with the .45. He'd had no idea it was coming. A Colt .45 automatic weighs about three pounds. I knocked the guy out cold. He fell in the alleyway. I stuffed the .45 in my pocket, grabbed Anvil Man up by the ankles, and started towing him lickety-split. Haymann appeared out of nowhere and gave me a hand. We dragged him up the front stairs unceremoniously as his head bounced against the steps, and we hauled him to the middle of the living room. Haymann cast a worried glance through the curtains.

"My reputation in the neighborhood is already not so great. I hope no one saw us."

"Nothing to do about it. Give me a hammer."

He scowled at me, then left the room and came back a few seconds later with a sledgehammer and a crowbar. I tore them from his hands.

"Hold on, Tarpon..."

I tossed the Polaroid on the table; Haymann glanced at it and vertical wrinkles appeared between his eyebrows. I searched Anvil Man. I found a Paraguayan passport and a driver's license in the name of Cedric Kasper, twenty-five hundred francs in hundred-franc bills and some change, and a CZ 52 pistol with three extra cartridges. Nothing else except a handkerchief. Cedric Kasper appreciated clean pockets. I kicked him in the nose. The pain brought him around. He opened his eyes without moving, gauged the situation, and readjusted his glasses, which were crooked. I knelt down on the floor near him, out of the way of a possible retaliation. I was holding the .45 in my left hand and the sledgehammer in the right. Haymann was sitting astride a chair near the table, waiting for whatever was going to happen next.

"You've got a nasty fracture," I said. "Those are the bones that take the longest to heal. Months at least. But with a little physical therapy afterward, you should be able to use both your hands in six months or so. Now" (I tapped his head with the hammer and he blinked) "you'd better tell me where Charlotte Malrakis is. Otherwise, I'm not the kind to torture someone, so I won't torture you, but I'll bust both your wrists. Given your line of work, I won't feel like I'm doing a bad deed, see? I'll simply bust your wrists, practically painlessly, very neatly and very permanently. Understand?"

"Yes."

He thought for a moment. Lying on his back, resting his

head on the floor, he looked quite relaxed. He was a real professional. I had no respect for him at all.

"I was wrong about you, Tarpon," he said at last. "We could use your talents. Of course, you'd make a lot more money."

He let out a sigh as he gazed at me. Then he told me where Charlotte was. Haymann had to go get a detailed map of the Paris region so that Kasper could show us exactly how to get there. He described the layout of the place and told us how many people there might be in the house. Haymann headed toward the door.

"We'll take my Aronde." (He went into the foyer and I heard him go upstairs.)

I took off my broken Kelton, tossed it in a corner, and put Kasper's watch—a gold Rolex—on my wrist. It was 2:35.

"How did you manage to get Charlotte Malrakis?"

"You're a solitary guy, Tarpon. With the exception of Haymann and that girl, you don't hang out with anyone."

You couldn't really say that I was *hanging out* with Charlotte Malrakis, but I didn't bother mentioning that.

"I first went to her place," said Kasper. "Your coat and jacket were there. Madrier didn't miss you by much."

"Why go to her place? Why not come here first?"

"Sheer chance. Maybe it was closer. In fact, I would've nabbed you if I hadn't been delayed by my arm and all that."

Haymann came back into the room with some wire, a pair of pliers, and a Beretta 12-gauge shotgun. We stood Kasper on his feet. We twisted his left arm behind his back and made him raise his right knee almost to his chin. Then we carefully tied him up in this position with the wire.

"Thanks. I'm so comfy now."

"Tell me about Fanch Tanguy."

"No way. For that, you'd have to torture me, Tarpon."

Fuck if he didn't smile at me then!

"If your brutes hurt the girl," I said, "I'll kill you later."

He looked at me without answering. He was still wearing a tiny smile.

Haymann had put on a hunting jacket. He left the house and pulled his Aronde out front. Hopping on one foot and leaning on the walls, Kasper managed to reach the door. We supported him as he walked down the three stairs. Haymann got behind the steering wheel. We settled Kasper in next to him. I sat in the back, with the shotgun on the floor. Haymann had the MR73 and I had the two pistols.

Haymann's Aronde is an old, run-down jalopy. We drove onto the ring road toward Porte de Vanves and then we eased onto the southern highway. It took us almost an hour to go the sixty kilometers to the exit at Achères-la-Forêt. Kasper was as quiet as a mouse. From time to time he twisted around a little and sucked air in through his teeth. The way he was tied up, you could be sure he wasn't having much of a good time.

When we got off the highway, I guided Haymann while looking at the map. We drove quickly past the house on a narrow forest road. It seemed that the place was the way Kasper had described it, an old gatehouse fifty meters from the road in the middle of a clearing of yellowing grass. We went a bit farther, six or seven hundred meters, left the road, and entered a woods where we parked. We attached Kasper with wire to the steering shaft, and we gagged him with adhesive bandages.

Haymann took a jerrican out of the trunk of the Aronde and put his shotgun through the handle. We went back to the gatehouse through the woods and reached the clearing from the side. At the edge of the woods, we stopped for a moment. I looked at Haymann and I was concerned.

"Don't worry about me," declared Haymann. "We'll do what we planned."

He started walking toward the house. He got to the door and knocked. With his cap, his hunting jacket, his shotgun, and his empty jerrican, he looked totally harmless and vaguely stupid. I had one knee on the ground and was aiming at the door with both hands on the CZ 52 as I leaned sideways against a tree trunk, just like they teach us in the refresher courses in the gendarmerie.

Nothing happened. At all.

Haymann knocked again. He secretly glanced my way with an anxious look in his eyes. We knew—we hoped we knew—that there were two guys in the place, one guarding Charlotte in a sort of workshop at the back of the building, the other in the main room onto which the door opened directly. The plan was simple and tasteful: hold a gun to the first guy so that he'd call out to the second.

Since there was no answer, Haymann with one hand still holding the jerrican, grabbed the doorknob with the other and opened the door partway, which was a huge mistake because both of his hands were full and he'd placed himself squarely in my line of fire. From where I was I could distinctly hear him say softly, "Anyone home?" and then I heard, and he heard it too, the clear, almost musical, frantic moan that Charlotte let out.

I groaned and ran toward the house, knocking over Haymann who, at the same time, was putting down his jerrican and pulling out his shotgun. I burst into the main room just as Charlotte was screaming again. Her cry was coming from upstairs and I took the steps four at a time. Haymann hurried behind me and we made quite a racket.

Meanwhile, the two characters in the bedroom only noticed us at the last minute, busy little bees that they were. The younger one, a small dark-haired guy with green eyes, wearing jeans and a turtleneck, was holding Charlotte by the ankles; her hands were cuffed to a pipe. The other guy, who must have been around forty, was stocky and almost bald with big yellow eyes in a ruddy face. When I entered the room, he was wearing only his shirt, his dick hanging out; his boxers and pants around his knees hindered his movements somewhat as he stepped to the side, grabbed a New Colt Python from a wicker chair, and aimed it at me.

Haymann fired over my shoulder. My hair was singed and I went completely deaf. The man in just his shirt spun around and dropped his revolver. He banged his forehead against the wall with a dull sound, bounced off it, and slid to the floor on his back. One of the two bullets had torn up his cheek but most of the spray had struck him above his left shoulder, shattering his collarbone. There was blood all over the place.

The little dark-haired guy let out a piercing cry and jumped, feetfirst, through the window.

I must have twirled three times around myself because too many things were happening at once and I'd lost my balance and my sense of direction. I think I wanted to thank Haymann because he'd probably saved my life, but just then he took a step forward, turned gray when he saw what he'd done, and fainted.

"Oh my God, my God, my God, my God, my God," Charlotte repeated mechanically, quickly, and ceaselessly from her knees on the floor, practically dislocating her neck to look at the room behind her.

Her voice seemed to come to me from afar. I walked over to the window. Down below there were shards of glass and pieces of broken window frame on the yellowing grass. I heard the sound of an engine and a Citroën CX 2000, which must have come out of a shed of some sort, went around the corner of the house. The little dark-haired one was at the wheel. It looked like he was bleeding too. And it sounded like the gearbox was grinding terribly while the car pogoed to the forest road, skidded as it turned into it, and disappeared. Besides shooting the little dark-haired guy in the back, there was nothing I could do, so I did nothing.

I turned back toward the room. I unbuttoned Haymann's shirt collar and gently slapped him. He opened his eyes and looked at me with hostility.

"Don't try to speak. Breathe deep. When you're able, sit up and place your head between your knees. It'll bring more blood to your brain."

My hearing came back to me. The guy in his shirt started to bellow. He mixed a variety of colorful insults and abject pleas with his cries of pain. Then he passed out. Lucky for him, Haymann was using bird shot. Still, the way the guy was bleeding was worrisome.

"Where's the key to the handcuffs?" I asked Charlotte and I had to grab her by the shoulders and shake her and repeat my question before she answered.

I took the key from the wounded guy's pants; I freed Charlotte. Haymann sat up, then stood; he stumbled and tried to cling to the wall.

"Head between the knees!" I shouted.

He obeyed. Charlotte got to her feet and rubbed her wrists.

"Where are your clothes?" I asked her.

"Downstairs."

"Go get dressed. Hurry. There's no one else in the house, is there? Besides those two, there was no one else?"

She shook her head. She seemed distracted. I tapped her on the shoulder.

"Go on."

She walked toward the door.

"Hey," I said (and I think I giggled nervously). "We got here just in time, didn't we?"

She gave me a stern glance over her shoulder. "Do you mean from the standpoint of sexual violence? No, Tarpon. You did not get here in time."

8

THE HOUSE consisted mainly of a common room with a cement workshop on the ground floor and three bedrooms upstairs. The furniture was rustic. There was a stuffed fox on the buffet in the main room, deer antlers in the bedrooms, and paintings of dogs, horses, stags, and game birds all over the place. I'd be lying if I said we went over the house with a fine-tooth comb. We went through it quickly. The guy in his shirt was bleeding out slowly in the bedroom. There was a phone downstairs that I used to call the gendarmerie in Fontainebleau. I told them to hurry, and to come with an emergency medical team.

Haymann and Charlotte left as I was starting to dial. When I hung up, I walked through the rooms again while I waited for them. Then the old Aronde pulled up in front of the house. I hurried toward the car and climbed in back. Haymann was at the wheel and Charlotte was next to him.

"Where's Kasper?"

Haymann took off.

"Escaped. It took us too long. He managed to wear down the wire. He can't be too far, because with a broken arm and two other limbs completely schwarz from numbness, you can bet he's in no shape to speed out of the area. The thing is, we don't have time to carry out a search if you called the gendarmes."

"I did call them."

The car crossed through Achères-la-Forêt, got on the local road, and headed toward the highway.

"What the fuck, Tarpon. Do *you* have string or rope at your place?"

"No," I answered.

"Well neither do I. I only had wire. Don't take it out on me."

"I didn't say anything," I said.

The Aronde got on the highway. We drove toward Paris. Haymann asked where we were going.

"We can go to my place," he said, "or else we can go to your place" (he glanced at Charlotte) "and then if the cops aren't there, we can wait for them. It's probably the best thing to do. I'm just asking."

"I know where we're going," said Charlotte. "It's a friend's place. I know where the key is, and he's in Ceylan."

"Perfect!" cried Haymann. "We'll go hide out there and with a little luck, we'll all have our pictures in the paper, who gives a shit, life has its ups and downs, as long as we're having a good time, all's well. Don't mind me if I'm a bit nervous."

"The guy won't die," I murmured. "I'm sure they're already giving him an emergency transfusion. He'll pull through."

"My uncle was at Drancy," said Haymann rather calmly. "His mother died while he was there. He asked—it's really amazing—he really and truly *asked* if they would let him out to go to the funeral, he swore to come right back. Listen up, that's not the funny part. Wait for it now. The guys authorized him to leave. Here it comes. He spent three days out of Drancy, and then he came back, he came back, he returned to Drancy. The guys were totally amazed to see him again. They sent him to Germany. And to the crematorium, the asshole. I prefer the next generation of Jews, you know. The ones who have automatic weapons and airplanes and barbed wire." (He laughed quietly.) "Shit, Tarpon, there were only ten years between me and my uncle, but I'm not a sheep, you know. I've used a gun and probably killed some Germans. I know how to use a shotgun. I was even a Marxist once. I've read Engels's *The Role of Force in History* and I remember it and I'm in total agreement with it. Shit."

"Would you like to pull over on the shoulder and I'll drive?" asked Charlotte.

"No thanks. I'm okay. I'll be okay."

None of us said another word for a while. As we neared Paris, following Charlotte's directions, we took the road that led east, and then the ring road up to Porte de Vincennes. Charlotte guided us until we reached a street near Place de la Nation. We found a spot and parked. It was almost 6:00 p.m. and there was a lot of traffic. It was raining and a cold wind was blowing.

Charlotte went to get the keys at the bakery on the corner where her friend left them whenever he was away. She made a stop at the newspaper stand and came back with *Le Monde* and the latest edition of *France-Soir*. We climbed two flights (no elevator). Charlotte was coughing, especially since she'd been smoking Haymann's filterless cigarettes for a while.

Charlotte's friend (whose name was Jules) had a very elegant three-room apartment cluttered with coffee tables, leather chairs, plastic things, chrome tubes, abstract paintings, and a profusion of exotic knickknacks.

"He's a filmmaker," Charlotte explained. "He makes short films, TV films, and lots of ads. He's into traveling. He counts both how many countries he's visited and how many he hasn't. Last I heard, he had nineteen to go, but he complains because new nations are constantly becoming independent. He's supposed to come back at the end of next week. We can relax."

She found an open carton of cigarettes and pulled out a pack. Haymann turned the portable radio on low. I searched inside *France-Soir* and managed to find five lines about a mysterious 2CV crushed during the night near Meulan, with a dead man inside. It didn't say that the vehicle belonged to me. As for the article SHOOTOUT IN LES HALLES, it was no longer on the first page and had shrunk by half. In *Le Monde*, there were eight lines about Madricr's death, and it said that the police were looking for me to question me.

"People are probably looking for all three of us," I said. "There's a group of tough guys who would love to skin us alive. And there are probably people in the police doing the same. And this whole story remains a total enigma to me, exactly like the curse of the pharaohs. Besides that, sweetie, everything's like you said. We can relax. Yeah."

We were in a sort of living room. I cleared the mess off the glass-topped coffee table and lined up various interesting objects in front of me: the .45 and its silencer; the Czech automatic (7.62 mm); the MR73; the Python that belonged to the man wearing just his shirt; the Beretta shotgun; the bullets that the man wearing just his shirt had in his pockets (357 Magnum, perfect for the MR73—with all the guns we'd collected, we'd finally found munitions that were compatible with one); and the shirt guy's wallet.

"I'm going to wash up."

"Is there anything to drink around here and can we help ourselves?" Haymann asked.

"Look in the kitchen. The side cabinet."

"Thanks."

Haymann left the room. I looked at Charlotte.

"I'm sorry," I said.

"I'm going to wash up," she repeated.

She left the room. After a moment I heard the water running noisily in the bathroom: she was going to take a bath. I loaded the MR73. Then I dumped the contents of the wallet on the coffee table. ID card in the name of Lionel Constantini, forty-four years old. Driver's license in the name of Antoine Chotard. Driver's license in the name of Louis Lopez. Car registration in the name of Antoine Chotard for a Peugeot 504. Health insurance card for the Solidarity and Foresight Insurance Company. Car insurance documents for the 504. Seventeen green points from Mobile. An illuminist and nutritional pamphlet printed on Bible paper and distributed by a certain Community of Reformed Skoptsy. It was folded in four, with on the right side a strange mixture of mystical and advertising idiocies, and on the left a series of numbers in pencil that looked like a telephone number. A credit card in the name of Louis Lopez. A membership card to the French Book Club in the name of Lionel Constantini. A benefactor membership card to the Stanislas Baudrillart Foundation. Two second-class subway-bus tickets. Three eighty-centime stamps. A bill from a mechanic for an oil change and lubrication for the 504. A calling card for a certain Renée Mouzon, bent and stained by having spent a long time in the wallet, with a telephone number added in red marker beneath the embossed name. That was all.

Haymann came back into the room with three empty glasses and a bottle of Bison vodka. He sighed as he sat down on the rust-colored leather couch, placed the glasses on the table, and poured himself something like twenty centiliters of vodka. Gesturing, he offered me the same. In return, I gestured similarly (on the one hand nodding my head, on the other holding my thumb and index figure quite close together), indicating that I would like some but less. Haymann poured.

"What time are we supposed to see your guy?"

"What guy?"

"Captain Melis-Sanz."

He looked completely lost for a second. Then he said, "Oh, yeah! Tonight. Sometime after seven, I suppose."

The water had stopped running in the bathroom. We heard a muffled crash coming from there, as if Charlotte had let the handheld showerhead fall. Haymann glanced over that way without turning his head.

"She's not gonna commit suicide, is she?" he asked.

"You're a real asshole," I said.

"Sorry."

He emptied his glass and poured in another twenty centiliters.

"Sorry," he said again.

"It's not worth dwelling on either. It was a nasty thing that happened. It's not something unimportant, but it's not a defilement either."

"Okay," said Haymann. "Okay, Tarpon. Don't get on your high horse."

"I'm not getting on my high horse!" I shouted and I closed my teeth over my glass and it broke. I spit the pieces of glass onto the carpet and hurriedly placed what was left of it on the coffee table; I'd spilled vodka everywhere. "Shit," I said.

Haymann carried away my broken glass, tossed it down the garbage chute, and came back with another glass. And served me.

"There's the problem of money," he said. "I have less than fifty francs on me. You?"

"I've got Kasper's twenty-five hundred and the six hundred or so that belonged to the guy you wounded. That'll last us a little while. Ready to go?"

"Ready."

Haymann emptied his glass. I went to knock on the bathroom door.

"Yes?"

"We're going out to do something," I shouted through the door. "We'll be back in an hour or two I hope. Rest up between now and then, okay?"

"Okay."

"See you."

"See you."

We took the Aronde. Night had completely fallen. It was still raining, windy, and freezing cold.

There were traffic jams and it took us almost twenty minutes to reach the neighborhood around Place de la Bastille and find a parking spot. On the fourth floor of a dilapidated building, Captain Melis-Sanz opened the door to us.

Captain Melis-Sanz was about sixty years old and five and a half feet tall. He had short legs, a wide torso, and a broad face topped with a thick, blond crew cut. He was wearing poor-quality jeans made in France, a checked cotton shirt frayed at the wrists and ragged at the collar, and a woolen jacket patched at the elbows. He and Haymann exchanged a few words in Spanish. The captain led us into a small room with sub-Lévitan furniture. We sat down on Formica chairs.

"I'll go get the man," said Melis-Sanz in a heavy accent as he looked at me. It sounded a little like "Yo go getta mahn."

"*Mouchasse graciasse*," I spluttered and, not having any other Spanish words in my vocabulary, I tapped the left side of my chest with my right palm. (I don't know if it was something about his eyes or what, but Captain Melis-Sanz created around us, in a radius of about thirty meters, an ambiance filled with different emotions: anger, despondency, and two or three other distressing feelings.)

He went out through a connecting door. I looked at Haymann who was gazing morosely at his fingernails. Melis-Sanz came back with a fellow who was even smaller than he was, completely bald, plump cheeks, mischievous eyes, a blue-gray suit made of thin material, and a cream-colored, open-necked nylon shirt. Haymann stood up and started speaking Spanish again. He and the bald guy tapped each other on the arms and shoulders with their palms, and then hugged each other, laughing in a sad way. At one point, the bald fellow shook my hand but no introductions were made.

We all sat down again and Melis-Sanz served us some anisette. We raised our glasses and drank very seriously. After a while, Melis-Sanz leaned forward and tapped me on the knee with his palm. Then he pointed to the bald fellow.

"He killed Tanguy." (His pronunciation was off, but I got it.)

I took the photo that Marthe Pigot had sent me out of my pocket. The bald guy nodded, smiling. I handed him the picture. He looked at it, handed it back to me, nodding and smiling and shrugging.

"Is it him or isn't it?" I asked.

"How should I know?" asked the bald guy, and the only accent his French had was one from the outskirts of Paris. "I don't remember the guy's face. It happened thirty years ago."

"Can you give me any details?" I asked. And I added, "Please."

"It was sheer chance. We'd stopped the car. At random. Two men inside, luggage in the back. One of the men fired at us. We fired back. The man was killed. We took the other one prisoner. We took the papers of both of them. The one who died was Fanch Tanguy. What other details do you want? There was money in the car, lots of dollars and pounds sterling. And gold coins and precious gems, too, and all kinds of jewelry. I remember that there were almost fifty gold wedding rings. But maybe they'd simply pillaged a second-hand jewelry store. We only took a little bit of it because we had to beat it and get farther up the mountain."

"And what allowed you to learn the dead man's identity? His papers?"

"As a matter of fact, there were several sets of papers. But he had documents from the German police in the name of Fanch Tanguy. And the guys in our group, French guys, said they recognized him from pictures they'd seen."

"Who was the other man?"

"No idea."

I raised my eyebrows.

"Even at the time we had no idea," the bald guy explained. "Because that guy also had several sets of false documents in the names of people no one knew. And unfortunately, he got away from us a few hours later, in the mountains. We didn't have time to interrogate him because we hadn't stopped moving since the exchange of gunfire, and there'd been a misunderstanding about guard shifts, and he escaped. It was night, it was the mountains . . ." (The bald guy sort of grinned and raised both palms horizontally.)

"Didn't you keep a regimental diary or something in

which the various identities of the two guys would've been written down?"

"Yeah, sure. But I've no idea where it is now."

"In Toulouse," said Melis-Sanz.

"I'm not sure about that."

"Sure!" stated Melis-Sanz, nodding energetically.

In any case, for the time being, Toulouse or Spitzberg, it was all the same to me. Nonetheless, the bald guy gave me an address in Toulouse. Melis-Sanz served us some more anisette; we drank it.

"Listen," I said as we were getting up to go, "isn't it possible that the guy who escaped was Fanch Tanguy? That he switched identities with the other guy, see what I mean?"

"No," said the bald guy, and then he hesitated, thought for a while, and shook his head. "No," he said. "Not possible. Oh, now that I think of it, and maybe it will help you, the other guy must have been a doctor. He had a medical bag with him, you know the kind."

I nodded noncommittally. Haymann and the bald guy gave each other taps on the shoulders again and kisses on the cheeks, there were handshakes all around, and Melis-Sanz walked us out to the landing. We left.

"Those guys, you know," said Haymann as we were walking to the car, "have practically never stopped fighting since 1933 or '34 in one way or another. But now we're old."

I didn't respond. It was dark and damp outside.

9

WHEN WE got back to Jules's apartment, Charlotte had straightened up the living room, set three places on the glass coffee table, and a mouthwatering aroma was wafting from the kitchen. The color television was on, broadcasting the end of the Channel 2 news. There was a story about a plane crash in which a French boxer had died, which seemed to call for detailed commentaries and lots of interviews. Charlotte came out of the kitchen dressed in a terry-cloth bathrobe three sizes too big for her, her hair under a sort of terry-cloth turban, and her cheeks pink from the steam.

"I went out to buy stuff to eat. I'm completely broke. Will roast chicken and potatoes do?"

We heartily approved. I picked up the phone and called Information. I had the name and number of the party and wanted to know their address. They gave it to me. The party in question, Renée Mouzon, lived in Neuilly. Thank you, Operator.

We sat at the table. The chicken was good. According to Charlotte, the most important thing was to stuff it with farmer's cheese. I wasn't thrilled with the idea, but the bird was incredibly tender, I had to admit.

"They mentioned you on the radio a while ago, Tarpon," Charlotte said. "They talked about the 2CV, the dead guy inside, and the bullet holes. They said 'bullet holes.' They said it was a nasty business."

"That's all?"

She nodded. After the news and the commercials, the anchor announced a film by Serge Cukor. ("George, idiot," Charlotte interjected calmly.) I wiped my mouth and got up.

"I think there's a phone booth downstairs not too far from here," I said. "Please excuse me for a moment."

"You're not leaving while a Cukor is on!" cried Charlotte with an expression of true horror on her face.

"I'd rather call from a booth," I said and went downstairs. I walked the two hundred meters to where I'd seen the phone booth and called the number.

"Hello?" (It was Coccioli and his mouth was full. I pushed the button and the call went through.)

"Eugène Tarpon speaking."

I distinctly heard swallowing and then Coccioli remained silent for three or four seconds.

"Better late than never," he said at last. "Where are you?"

"Tsk, tsk, tsk."

"What is it you want?"

"Where are *you*? What the heck is this phone number?"

"I'm up shit's creek," he chuckled nervously. "No, it's my number, just a local joke, I'm home. Square Saint-Lambert, in the fifteenth arrondissement. Do you want the address?"

I stupidly shook my head no, all alone in the dark in my lit-up phone booth, with the rain drumming on the windows.

"No. Do you have a car? What does it look like?"

"GS. Tobacco colored."

"Give me the license plate number."

He gave it to me.

"Okay," I said. "Get in it right now. Take the ring road near Porte de Versailles. Drive at fifty kilometers an hour in the right lane. Keep driving around Paris and wait until I signal you."

"Whaaat? Listen, Tarpon, that's not happening."

"Yes, it is," I said, and I hung up.

At around 9:15 in the evening there aren't a ton of tobacco-colored Citroën GSs driving slowly in the right lane of the ring road; ordinarily, there isn't even one. When Coccioli's came into view, approached the bridge at Porte de Vincennes, and drove over it, I was on the bridge looking out for it and getting soaked. And I saw it.

I went back to the Aronde that was parked about a hundred meters from there, its engine still warm. I got into it, started it up, pulled onto the ring road, and followed Coccioli. Haymann's Aronde is a very mediocre old beater, but it can go up to almost a hundred kilometers an hour if you hold on tight. I even passed an SM, but I have to admit it was going really slowly.

I caught up to Coccioli near Porte de la Villette. First I pulled up behind him to check the license plate. Then I flashed my headlights twice. He lit the light inside his car and briefly turned around to look at me. I passed him and then pulled in front of him at half speed. The Porte de la Villette exit ramp appeared before us; I put on my blinker and took the ramp. Coccioli followed.

We parked on that avenue that has loads of restaurants with good meat. I walked toward Coccioli's car. He got out. He was wearing an overcoat and his eyes were hollow.

"No point standing here freezing off our..." I remarked.

We went into a greasy spoon and sat down in the back, Coccioli with a cup of coffee and me with a hot toddy.

"So," I said, "you're double-dealing."

"Me?" said Coccioli. "What do you mean? Of course not!"

"Yeah, right. While you were looking for me at Haymann's, someone else was looking for me at Charlotte Malrakis's. Division of labor."

"You're nuts."

"But on the other hand," I continued, "you more or less warned me about Madrier. I even believe you may have saved my life, although perhaps not on purpose. So all this isn't very coherent. Unless one supposes you're trying to have it both ways. Or else I'm too suspicious. You didn't like Madrier, and maybe you don't like anyone with ties to him. But they're powerful people. Maybe you'd like to eradicate them. But you're not sure if it can be done. So you're giving me a hand so I can eradicate them. But if I fuck it up, you'll help them finish me off. You just want to find yourself on the winning side. Any comments?"

"Just wait a second. It's not like that," said Coccioli. "Wait just one second."

He was looking at the table. I drank half of my toddy and burned my esophagus.

"Oh, what the hell," Coccioli declared. "Believe whatever you want. I don't give a damn."

I stared at him. I hadn't managed to make him angry. There were several explanations for this, none pleasant.

"What do you know about Fanch Tanguy?" I asked.

"Before you showed me that photo, I'd never even heard his name."

"You oughta read up on the history of the Collaboration. It would be useful in your line of work."

"Oh, it's so easy to spit on the cops."

"Sadly, that's true."

Coccioli pulled on a strand of his black hair, dragging it in front of one eye. It made him cross-eyed.

"What went down in Marseilles?" I asked. "What did the financial division of the regional police discover that forced it to disband and give everyone a promotion?"

"That makes no sense," Coccioli said thoughtfully.

"What doesn't make sense?"

"Look, I don't know what they discovered, what Madrier might have discovered. He's the one who found something, and there may be two or three other cops who know what it was. As for me, I have no idea and I don't understand." (Since I was making nasty faces at him, he shook his head briskly and sat up straight; his hair whipped across his face.) "Look," he said again, "I know what Madrier was working on, but it doesn't make sense, because if he'd succeeded, it wouldn't have been covered up."

"What was it?" I asked patiently, pronouncing my words calmly and precisely. "What on earth was it that Madrier was working on?"

"The opposition's money," answered Coccioli.

"What?"

"The dough and where certain guys, certain groups, and certain companies who support the opposition parties to the government got it from. That's why it doesn't make any sense. If Madrier had found the information he'd been looking for, you can be sure that the government would've used it."

"And how do you know it didn't?"

"What?"

I let my eyes wander around the dining room. Across the painted wood partition and the frosted glass, fat men were laughing at the bar. The place smelled of dirty frying oil.

"Oh, yeah, I see," Coccioli said suddenly.

I took a Gauloise from the pack he'd placed on the table and lit it with his lighter.

"Do you know who Kasper is?" I asked.

"Yeah. Okay. I know who he is."

"Do you know where he is?"

"No."

"Can you find out?"

"No."

I stubbed out the barely started Gauloise. "You don't have, let's say, intimate ties with them."

"One could even say I don't have any ties at all."

"One could, but it wouldn't be true."

"Look, Tarpon," said Coccioli, "stop bugging me. You don't know how the game is played. We're among policemen, we're among comrades, there are some things . . . Listen, the police are doing their job; and then small cliques form, because the work isn't always clean, and so these cliques form among people who have the same skeleton in the same closet. You can understand that, can't you, for God's sake? And those on the outside of the clique know a little about what's going on, but it stops there. No one even bothers to truly know who's in and who's out of the clique."

"So you don't even know if you, personally, Coccioli, are in or out. How convenient."

Coccioli brought his coffee to his lips and I heard his teeth bump against the cup. A tiny stream of coffee flowed down his chin. He banged his cup on the table.

"I know my place, Tarpon," he said. "There'd be no point in explaining it to you."

"As for me," I said calmly, "there is not a single cop I can call on at this time. There might be only five or six cops in all of France who are mixed up enough in this to want to kill me if I find them, but that's all it takes. I can't go to the police. I'm sure that a guy like Commissioner Chauffard, for example, is clean, because they took the investigation away from him. Still, if I go to him, he'll start by locking me up. He'd have to. And when I'm locked up, anything could happen to me. I could hang myself in my cell or something. Or suppose I were to go to Internal Affairs—"

"It's not a good idea to get Internal Affairs involved in this shitstorm," Coccioli interrupted sharply, and I saw his lips purse.

"Suppose I were to do it. They'd also lock me up. And if your jokers have political protection, I'm even afraid of Internal Affairs. You're one lucky guy. I'm gonna keep on running until I'm caught." (I finished my hot toddy, which was no longer hot.) "I want Charles Pradier's police file. I want Kasper's too, if he has one. I want you to look in the archives for me, Coccioli. I want you to learn as much as you can about Fanch Tanguy, and about Madrier's past. Do whatever it takes. I'll get back to you. Stay seated while I leave."

I stood up.

"By the way, why aren't you even trying to arrest me?" I asked.

"Good question," Coccioli sighed.

He practically smiled at me, the bastard! I walked across the dining room and went out onto the avenue. It was still raining. I looked around me. It was around 10:00 p.m. and traffic was light.

I walked across the shiny pavement and got back behind the wheel of the Aronde, grumpy. I was tired, my ribs and hips were sore, my side hurt, I was irritated and I'd had enough. For a second I thought about going back to Coccioli and turning myself in and goodbye and good luck. I started the car.

I made a U-turn and headed toward the ring road. A Citroën SM pulled out and made a U-turn behind me. I took the outer ring road. The SM followed me. I was going eighty kilometers an hour. It was going eighty. From my sheepskin jacket (actually, Nick Malrakis's sheepskin jacket), I took out the MR73. I placed it on the seat next to me.

I drove by several exits that led to Paris and the SM didn't move any closer to me. I was going to have to lose them or else let them tail me until I led them to Haymann and Charlotte. I didn't know how to lose them with the Aronde.

It took me until I got to Porte Brancion to make up my mind. Then I put on my blinker and turned onto the long ramp that heads up toward the railroad bridge. Once I got to the top, with the SM eighty to a hundred meters behind me, I saw that the crossroad in front of the bridge was blocked by a police van and motorcycles. The police were dangling huge red blinking lanterns in front of them to stop the cars.

I don't know what I would've done if I'd thought about it, but I noticed I was speeding up as I reached them and they got out of the way, scurrying left and right. I drove through the roadblock. The Aronde was doing almost a hundred kilometers an hour. I ran two red lights, gripping my steering wheel, and now the SM was on my tail. It had also driven through the roadblock and run two red lights, and then there were two motorcycles behind the SM, so I sped down the entrance ramp to the ring road at Porte de Vanves. When I got to the bottom, I turned the steering wheel a little and put on the hand brake, and the Aronde spun around.

I accelerated. I found myself heading west, quickly, against the traffic on the outer ring road. It was obvious to me that I was fucked and I thought about the situation with a certain amused curiosity. In the meantime, someone had started shooting; I didn't know for sure at what or at whom, but there was at least one machine gun. And I was going down the ring road against traffic with headlights coming at me, zigzagging like mad, and passing me on the right and left like snowballs, in a pandemonium of brake lights. I had a laughing fit.

After, I rammed into the median barrier. I bounced around for quite a while and finally stopped in a haze of burned rubber. Without thinking I stuffed the MR73 in my pocket, opened my door, and got out on the roadway a bit distracted (I wasn't really sure what I was doing, know what I mean?) and I walked onto the median island, sheltered from the cars that continued to fly down the road, but a little more slowly— there was a bottleneck forming between Porte Brancion and Porte de Vanves, and I could still hear shots but no one was shooting at me. I leaned against the median barrier. I'd stopped laughing but my knees were trembling uncontrollably. I was waiting to be led to prison or maybe to the slaughterhouse. I think I was a bit tired.

10

AFTER a moment, let's say somewhere between forty seconds and a minute, I realized no one was bothering with me at all. What's good about the ring road is that it's lit up: I looked toward the Porte de Vanves. There were now cars stopped along two or three hundred meters and, at the head of the traffic jam, I could vaguely make out the SM. It had rammed the central median and all its windows were shattered. There were policemen on the ramp. Shots had stopped ringing out. Since it's my job to understand everything, I understood that the SM had attempted to take the same turn as I had, and missed. And then I thought maybe the cops had fired at the SM, or else the people in the SM had fired at me, and the cops thought that it was at them, or who knows.

I looked up and saw I was under the bridge. Actually, I was under two bridges because I was under city traffic, which was itself under a railroad bridge. The police blockade was over my head. I walked across the inner ring road, westward. I got to the bottom of the access ramp to Porte Brancion. I took the ramp. No one was there to interrogate me or fire at me. It was restful.

On the other hand, there was quite a crowd on the level of city traffic: stopped cars, rubberneckers, and cops running in every direction.

"What's going on?" a little old man with a leashed dog

asked me. He was wearing a dirty beret with a brownish cigarette butt in his mouth. His tone was sullen and disaffected.

"I don't know. It's over that way." (I pointed toward Porte de Vanves, to the other side of the railroad bridge.) "I think there was an accident."

"Gunshots!" the old guy exclaimed dryly. "I heard gunshots!"

"Don't ask me," I said. "I just got here."

He shrugged. I walked around him and headed north. He followed me with his eyes. I took the Métro at the Porte de Vanves stop. I got back to Jules's place around 11:00 p.m. Haymann was in the living room, on the leather couch, reading Jack London's *John Barleycorn* and sipping from a large glass of pink vodka. The radio was playing softly on the glass coffee table.

"I wouldn't mind a glass myself," I remarked.

"I finished the vodka," said Haymann. "There's scotch in the kitchen. The girl's gone to bed," he added because I was looking around questioningly. "She was exhausted. You look exhausted too."

I nodded and went to make myself a scotch and water, very diluted, that I brought into the living room. I sat down with a grunt of satisfaction.

"I wrecked your car."

"Oh," said Haymann.

I filled him in on the details.

"How is it they were waiting for you outside the café?" Haymann asked. "Coccioli didn't have time to warn them, did he?"

"I don't know. I think they were just tailing Coccioli."

"Okay," said Haymann. "On the other hand, maybe he's

been with them since Marseille, since the beginning. When he sent Marthe Pigot to you, he specifically told you not to do the investigation she wanted."

"Normal, given the circumstances."

"Still, lucky for him."

I sighed.

"You know," Haymann said, "this can't go on much longer."

"I know."

"It's a miracle they haven't nabbed you already. You're gonna need a miracle every day to continue to run. And exactly where are you planning on running to?"

I shrugged and sighed again and picked up the phone. I took a slip of paper from my pocket, consulted it, and dialed a number. The exchange seemed to belong to someone living outside of Paris.

"Well," said Haymann stiffly, "do whatever you want."

It took quite a while for me to be connected.

"Community of Reformed Skoptsy," said a smooth, feminine voice. "How may I help you?"

I hung up. I stood and walked toward the bookcases. I looked in the big color *Larousse* dictionary, in the *Petit Robert* dictionary, and in *Chambers Twentieth Century Dictionary*, but it wasn't in there.

"What are you looking for?" asked Haymann.

I handed him the mystico-nutritional pamphlet. "Skoptsy."

"If memory serves," said Haymann, "it's a very old Russia sect. Cheerful bunch. They believed that evil came from the flesh, and they had a certain propensity to rip off their gonads while singing hymns. Thinking about joining the order, Tarpon, old man? It looks like you've got a phone number in the Seine-et-Marne region there, but I wouldn't swear to it."

I called Information. Since I had the name and number

of what I was looking for, good old Information had no trouble giving me the address. The Community of Reformed Skoptsy perched near Villers-Cotterêts. I thanked Information, hung up, and wrote down the address.

"Speaking of gonads," said Haymann, "you missed something. You'd have been better off sitting in front of the TV instead of playing daredevil. That Ava Gardner, my God, what a beauty! Now what are you looking for?"

"A road map."

"No can do. We'll buy one tomorrow."

"And a car, while we're at it. If they still don't mention you in the papers, you'll go to some junkyard or other and by us a clunker. We can't afford anything better. As long as it lasts a few days, that's all I ask."

"At your service, boss!" Haymann declared. "Look, can we stop talking shop for now? I'm a bit sad and a bit weary, Tarpon. Want me to teach you to play Chinese chess?" (I shook my head.) "There's not just Western chess in this house," said Haymann, "there's also Japanese chess and Chinese chess. Our Charlotte knows how to play Chinese chess. She beat me, the little devil. She's a sweetheart."

"Yeah."

"Too skinny. I prefer Ava Gardner. But she's a sweetheart. You should go wish her good night. I think she'd like that."

"What the ... ?" I muttered. "What? Of course not!"

I turned back toward the bookcases and began looking at the different titles on the spines. I heard Haymann chuckle quietly behind me, then I heard him empty his glass, put it back down, and stand up, sighing.

"I made up a bed for myself in the other bedroom," he said. "Sorry, old man, but you've got the couch. Sweet dreams and don't bother looking for the scotch. I'm taking it with me."

"Good night," I said.

"Good night."

I remained a moment looking at the books' spines. I felt exhausted, and yet I was not sleepy at all. After a while, I slipped back into the sheepskin jacket and left the apartment.

I took the Métro at Nation and got out at Sablons. Renée Mouzon lived on a small street two hundred meters from the Métro, in an upscale building. Outside the concierge's door was a list of residents, very neatly printed, with the name of each person on a small detachable rectangle. I took the elevator to the fifth floor, where there were two double doors. On one of the doors was a calling card in the name of Renée Mouzon, identical to the card I'd found in the wallet of the man in his shirt. It was 11:45. I rang the doorbell, leaving my finger on it until someone opened. It didn't take long.

"What is it?"

The woman had opened the door just a slit. There was a chain lock on it, a rather useless thing. I took an old card out of my pocket and flashed it in front of her eyes.

"Internal Affairs of the National Gendarmerie," I announced, as seriously as possible. "Renée Mouzon? Open the door, please."

She looked at me wearily and opened the door. She led me into a Louis XV living room with ivory-colored drapery. She was wearing a silk bathrobe; on her feet were slippers with white pompons. Her hair was as curly as a sheep's and the color of fresh butter. She had a nice body, a bit worn, voluptuous, that wiggled beneath the silk as she walked, and a round, pretty face, milky and a bit worn as well, and large blue droopy eyes. She kept her cigarette with its cork tip in her mouth as she spoke.

"You know," I said as we were entering the Louis XV

living room, "you don't have to let me in at this hour. But it would put us behind schedule if I were obliged to come back tomorrow."

"Sit down."

"Thank you for your cooperation," I said and I sat down carefully in a wing chair.

Renée Mouzon stubbed out her cigarette in a porcelain ashtray, took another one from a silver box, and lit it with a silver lighter.

"Are you here about Lionel?" she asked.

"Who's Lionel?"

"Oh! For God's sake!" she cried with a vehemence that surprised me. "Don't play games with me!" (She took a step to the side, crossed her ankles, and stumbled; she fell seated in an armchair with such lightness and grace that her movements seemed almost voluntary and choreographed.) "I know he's a bandit," she declared. "I don't give a damn. He's my guy."

She glared at me, daring me to say otherwise. Then she giggled quietly and leaned forward (displaying the top of her breasts) to pick up a silver goblet and a crystal carafe from the floor next to the armchair.

"Do you want some?" she asked, waving the objects in my direction. "It's rum," she explained.

I shook my head. "Are we speaking about Lionel Constantini?"

"*Now* what did he do?" She poured herself a full goblet of rum, holding the goblet and carafe up to her eyes. The smoke from her cigarette caused her right eyelid to flutter.

"He was mixed up in a shootout in the Fontainebleau Forest," I said and she put the carafe back down hard and looked at me anxiously.

"He...he's okay?" she asked. "He's not wounded or... or...?"

"I..." (I licked my lips, looking glum.) "Nothing serious..."

She leapt from her chair, rushed at me, almost fell to the floor, and grabbed me by the collar. She practically lifted me off the ground; in any case, I found myself standing, cornered against the wing chair. Renée Mouzon stank of rum. She hadn't dropped her goblet, so she threw half of its contents on my jacket.

"Where is he? Tell me where he is!" (She was screaming.)

"If you let go of me and answer a few questions, I'll tell you how to reach him."

She dropped the goblet and it bounced against the rug. Whatever was left of the rum spilled all over. She shook me like a plum tree, holding tightly to my collar in a way that was, shall I say, methodical.

She walked backward dragging her feet and sat down in the armchair.

"I'm truly sorry to do this," I said. "But I must."

"Bastard," she said calmly and softly.

"Do you know someone named Fanch Tanguy?" (She shook her head, her eyes empty.) "What about Charles Pradier?"

"He's dead." (Feeble, mournful voice.)

"You knew him?"

"He was a friend of Lionel's. I met him two or three times."

"Did he and Lionel work regularly together?"

"I don't know."

"Every now and then?"

"I don't know. Maybe." (Voice still feeble.)

"Were they working together recently?"

"I think so."

"Why do you think so?"

"Huh? Oh, Lionel was here last night, and he got a phone call, and then he told me Charles Pradier was dead."

"And what were they working on together these past few days?"

"I don't know. Lionel doesn't talk about his business with me."

"He could've let something slip."

She laughed under her breath. She grabbed the carafe of rum and drank straight from it. Rum dribbled down her chin and through the opening in her bathrobe. When she put the carafe down, she laughed out loud, her mouth wide open.

"You're destroying yourself," I remarked, "by falling in love with guys like that and hitting the sauce the way you're doing."

She looked at me as if I'd come from Mars.

"I believe I've nothing more to say to you," she declared. "In any case, you're lying to me. I don't believe that Lionel is dead."

"Lionel is in the hospital in Fontainebleau. He was hit in the shoulder with lead shot. He lost some blood, but he'll be okay pretty soon."

"Are you sure?"

"I swear."

"Good," said Renée Mouzon after a moment of reflection. "Okay, I believe you."

"I have to finish questioning you," I said, "and then you'll be authorized to call Fontainebleau."

"Three questions."

"Excuse me?"

She giggled. Her head was bobbing. "You're a nice little

bastard," she said as way of explanation. "You've got three questions, like in a fairy tale. And then I won't say another thing."

I stared at her. She was still giggling. I sighed.

"Do you know someone named Kasper?"

"No. One down."

"What is the Community of Reformed Skoptsy?"

"It's some kind of fake monastery near Meaux. It's supposed to regenerate body and mind. You get the type. Yoga and meditation. Big bosses and old hags. That's where I met Lionel. But hold on, Lionel isn't the kind who believes in that sort of nonsense, and neither am I. My boss was spending some time there, and I, well, I'm his secretary, see, and Lionel had a meeting with my boss there, that's all. Okay, two down, one to go."

I was thinking desperately about my third question, because I had a definite sense that she was going to do what she'd said—not say another word after she'd given me her third answer. But my mind was empty, or maybe it was too full.

"What does your boss do?" I asked foolishly.

"He's the director of an association for the blind," Renée Mouzon said, and then she added, "That's three." As her head fell to the side, her mouth opened slightly and emitted a gentle snore; she was out like a light.

I I

As I was closing the front door to Jules's apartment, Charlotte ran toward me.

"Where on earth have you been? You scared me half to death, idiot!"

"Sorry," I said, and I walked around her into the living room where I took off the sheepskin jacket and sat down on the couch to try to think.

Charlotte followed me and perched on a white plastic bucket seat with a bright orange cushion atop a rather high pedestal. She was wearing one of Jules's sweaters, a monstrous, wide-ribbed, white linen thing that fell practically to her knees. She was glaring at me. She was smoking a Gitanes and there was a pile of cigarette butts in a square ashtray on the glass table. The room was filled with smoke.

"I was worried sick," Charlotte said. "I had a nightmare and then I couldn't fall back asleep, and you weren't here anymore."

"Well, hey!" I shouted, somewhat incoherently. "Where's this guy Nick? Where's your husband? I mean—"

"He's shooting a movie down south. Your association of ideas is interesting, Tarpon."

"Huh?"

"I say I can't sleep and all of a sudden you ask me where my guy is. He's not my guy, by the way."

"Not your guy?"

"Nick's a prick. I don't give a damn. He can go wherever he wants with his whores. Just let it drop, Tarpon."

"I'm letting it drop," I said. "I didn't say anything. You're the one—"

"Shut up a minute, will you, Tarpon!"

I sighed, lowered my eyes, and remained motionless for a few moments. I could hear Charlotte moving about on her chair. Apparently she was trying to find a comfortable position and couldn't.

"I went to Renée Mouzon's place," I said. "You know, the woman whose address I found in the wallet, the wallet of the guy Haymann wounded."

I started telling Charlotte about it. After three sentences, she left her perch and came to curl up at one end of the sofa, swearing and cursing at the chair and saying she would be more comfortable on the couch. I got up to open the window and let some air in, and then I sat down in the armchair.

"Chicken," Charlotte hissed at me.

I took no notice and finished my story. I added a few comments and speculations. Charlotte went to close the window; it was getting cold.

"Tomorrow," I said, "if we don't all have our kissers in the papers, old man Haymann will try to get us a car. Among other things, I'd like to check out the Seine-et-Marne region."

"Yeah. Me too."

"Oh no you don't," I said. "You're going to stay put in this apartment until this business is over."

"No way. I'm afraid when I'm by myself."

"Sweetheart, I'm serious."

"I'll do whatever I want," Charlotte declared. "Either you keep me with you, or else I'll go to the papers and tell them everything. Just watch the shit hit the fan. Anyway, that's what we should do, if you ask me. But you don't like the idea."

I thought and sighed. "Let's sleep on it. It's two in the morning and we've had a rough day. Time to go to sleep."

"Good idea," said Charlotte. "Come to bed."

"Go to bed," I said.

"Come to bed."

I looked at her. She giggled.

"That's enough now, Charlotte!" I said.

"Why? Do you have a valid objection? Give me one valid objection."

I really tried to find one. "I'm not good-looking," I said.

"I'll be the judge of that. If you don't find me attractive, that's something else. Tell me you don't find me attractive."

"I don't find you attractive."

"Fucking liar," said Charlotte.

"Oh, what the hell," I said and stood up. "What the hell. All right."

She went into the back bedroom. I followed her. I undressed, embarrassed, in the half-light and then I went to join Charlotte in bed. Immediately she drew me to her with strength and spontaneity, and a great deal of nervousness. After a moment she pulled away vehemently; in fact, she punched me in the eye as she pushed me away, rolled out of bed, and ran from the bedroom into the bathroom where I heard her vomiting.

When she came out, I'd put on a pair of pajamas I'd found in the bedroom closet and was sitting in the living room. I'd also found a blanket that I'd brought in and placed on the couch.

"I'm terribly embarrassed," Charlotte said softly. "It's not you, you know. It's those guys. They've really shaken me up, despite everything. I'd really like to sleep with you—I'm sure it would be great. In a little while, a day or two, okay?"

"Whenever you'd like, yes, sure," I said softly as well. I took her by the elbow and led her to the bedroom, helped her change into pajamas, put her in bed, tucked her in, and gently stroked her hair. She fell asleep quickly.

I left the bedroom door ajar in case Charlotte had more nightmares. I went into the bathroom and washed my socks and shirt. I hung them up to dry. As far as the shirt went, it was sort of a waste of time because of the burn and tear on the side, but I needed something clean for tomorrow. Then I took a shower and went to lie on the living-room couch under the blanket at around 3:30 in the morning. I fell asleep immediately and woke up at noon.

A sound of hushed voices was coming from the kitchen. I went toward it, rubbing my eyelids with my fists. I was appalled that it was so late. At the same time, I was pretty happy that I'd slept so long—I felt nicely rested and my various bruises seemed much better.

In the kitchen, Haymann and Charlotte were sitting at the table in front of the morning papers, smoking as they talked heatedly. Charlotte kissed me on both cheeks and Haymann started making more coffee in a Cona coffeemaker. Charlotte had brought back a ton of croissants when she'd gone to get the papers. I was starving. I wolfed down some croissants while leafing through the dailies. Our photos were nowhere to be found. All the front pages were filled with the story about the boxing champion who'd died in the plane crash, or else with political news. In the back pages, new sordid stories seemed to have replaced ours in the public's interest.

There was, however, a story about a shootout on the ring

road and some mysterious tragedy in the Fontainebleau Forest. In the first story, it seemed that the police had apprehended some "habitual offenders" who were trying to break through a roadblock (their names were unfamiliar to me). In the second, a hunting shotgun had wounded another "habitual offender." No link was established between the two affairs; the second one was briefly mentioned in less than six lines in only one paper, and nowhere was there mention of me, nor of the "disappearance" of Charlotte or Haymann.

"The press is corrupt," Charlotte affirmed. "They're blacking out information."

"It's the cops who're doing the blackout," Haymann responded dryly. "The press is doing its job."

"Yeah, right."

"Listen, let's not start that again."

"Yeah. Don't start that again, please. We've got enough on our plates."

A little while later, we left the apartment. Haymann went off toward Porte d'Orléans and Highway 20, hoping to find on the way, in some not too far suburb, a car salesman of the kind of car about to go to the scrapyard. Charlotte and I headed for the Métro at Saint-Augustin, near where the Stanislas Baudrillart Foundation for the Blind was located.

For once it wasn't raining, but the sky was gray and cloudy, and the wind biting. I'd discovered that Jules was about my size and I'd borrowed one of his pink shirts. I don't think he had a single plain white shirt.

The Stanislas Baudrillart Foundation sat right next to the Saint-Augustin church on a small street on the third floor of a posh building. On the street corner was a run-down café from where we could see the building entrance. Charlotte was fooling with her sunglasses.

"What if I put them on? I promise I could pass for a blind woman. I'm an actress, Tarpon."

"We already discussed that. These people see blind folk all fucking day. Let it go. We'll do as we planned."

Charlotte grumbled and shrugged. She crossed the street and headed toward the entrance of the building. I went into the café and ordered a coffee at the counter. Through the window I saw Charlotte enter the building. It was 2:30 in the afternoon. At 3:10 I saw Renée Mouzon arrive in a taxi. At 3:25 Charlotte came back out.

"It wasn't easy," she said when she joined me at the counter. "I really had to do a song and dance. I said I wanted to speak to the director, that I wouldn't leave without having seen him and that I didn't want to say about what. Luckily it's a charitable institution. Everyone was very patient. When I finally said I was just looking for work, they weren't too happy."

"But did you see the guy?"

"Yeah, in the end, for two minutes. A very polite guy, as a matter of fact. He explained nicely that there were no openings and, in any case, the pay was bad. The well-paid jobs are reserved for the visually impaired. That's how he put it. And it's true. Out of the three women I saw, two were blind. And you were right to send me in instead of going yourself. I also saw your fat blondie."

"Renée Mouzon."

"Yeah, she's the guy's secretary, a fat bleached blond with little pig eyes, dressed all in white. She looked like a white elephant."

"What about the director? What did you think of him?"

"Handsome. Around forty, brown hair, tall, tan. His name is Georges Rose. It said so on his door."

"It was written on his door, not 'it said so,'" I corrected her.

Charlotte looked at me, wide-eyed. "What an asshole you are!" she cried.

"Would you recognize Georges Rose if you saw him again?"

"Relax. It's true, you know, you're an asshole."

"Well then," I said, "let's just wait."

We ordered two more coffees and sat down at a small table in the café's small dining room. Charlotte gave me a sidelong glance.

"You know, Tarpon, it was stupid to come at two thirty in the afternoon. Four thirty would've been fine. We've now got at least an hour to kill. Did you ever have so much downtime on other investigations?"

"Of course."

"At the movies?"

I shrugged.

"We could've stayed in the apartment. Both of us. Comfortably. Until three or four."

"You're not going to psychoanalyze me again, are you?" I asked.

"I like you, Tarpon. You're a riot."

"You know," I said, "when things have calmed down, I'd be more than happy to have an affair with you."

Charlotte burst out laughing and raised her arms in the air. "An affair!" she repeated.

Just then, Haymann came into the café. He was an hour early.

"Oh," he said, "you're here. Am I interrupting something?" (He stared at us, turning his head back and forth several times.)

"Everything's fine," I said. "You're early."

"I found one right away." (He sat down and waved two

fingers toward the waitress.) "An Alfa Romeo. Six hundred and fifty francs. It's about fifteen years old and was in a serious accident. The body could fall apart under our asses at any time." (He turned toward the waitress.) "A beer and a cognac. Apparently it can go up to a hundred and fifty kilometers an hour. We should try it, just for the thrill of it."

"We can't be seen from outside, I trust?" I asked, nodding toward the window.

"No." (Haymann grabbed the cognac from the waitress before she had time to set it on the table.) "I parked the damn jalopy on the corner and simply came in here to throw one back. I thought you'd be out walking while you waited for me." (He downed his cognac and grabbed the beer with his left hand even before the right one had come down.)

"It's not good weather for walking around," Charlotte declared, bristling. "It's weather for staying warm. In bed!"

"I bought a can of black paint and some decals," Haymann said as he put down his empty beer glass. "We'll have to change the plates when we can. Obviously I had to give my name. In twenty-four hours, they'll be looking for those plates. Waitress!" he cried, lifting two fingers.

"What the fuck are you doing with a weapon?" I hissed— Haymann's jacket had fallen open when he'd leaned forward and I could see the grip of the Python between his shirt and his trousers.

"I took it this morning."

"Don't wear it like that. You're gonna blow your balls off. At least put it in your jacket pocket. How much do I owe you?" I asked the waitress.

"Wait a sec. I'm gonna have another small one."

"Here comes the director," Charlotte announced calmly.

12

DIRECTOR Georges Rose was a tall, tan, handsome man in his forties, as Charlotte had said. Maybe just past forty; his hair was very black, probably dyed at the temples, and his skin was leathery. Must have been a fan of sun lamps. And of yoga, the sauna, and all that sort of thing. Yeah, it made sense.

He walked out of the building looking very busy, wearing an overcoat and a fedora, both of which were navy blue, and carrying a Delsey briefcase. Renée Mouzon was trotting behind him. She wore a white raincoat with a rabbit-fur collar and was carrying a handbag. Even from fifty meters away and through a dirty window, you could see that she was overly made-up, and she looked distraught. She held a handkerchief in her left hand and was biting on it while Rose, standing firmly on the sidewalk, glanced furiously up and down the street, looking for, it seemed, a vehicle that wasn't there.

Just then a metallic-gray Peugeot 504 appeared on the corner, drove down the street at half speed, and double-parked in front of Rose. The guy at the wheel had on a chauffeur's cap. He was on the small side with a round face and a waxy complexion. His neck was shaved, and you couldn't see any hair at all under his cap. I had the feeling I'd already seen him but that didn't seem possible. Sitting to his right was Cedric Kasper.

Rose and Renée Mouzon immediately walked over to the car. The chauffeur opened the back door for them without getting out, and the director and his secretary got in as the 504 took off in a hurry.

Haymann, Charlotte, and I were much too slow. As Georges Rose was leaving his building, we were just paying our bill, and when the 504 pulled up, we were walking toward the café door. With Renée Mouzon and Kasper involved, there was no longer any possible way for us to show our mugs in public.

As soon as the 504 started heading toward the end of the road, Haymann rushed outside and ran toward the end of the street, with Charlotte and me on his heels. The 504 turned and disappeared just as Haymann was opening the door of a horrible bottle-green Giulia whose four fenders and doors were covered with rust and some brownish coating.

"Hand over the keys," I ordered Haymann. "You and the girl, go back to the apartment and stay there."

"You actually think there's something to discuss here?" asked Haymann, settling in behind the wheel and starting the engine (at the same time, Charlotte got in back).

"Jean-Baptiste!" I cried.

"We'll leave without you, Eugène," Haymann threatened.

I gave in with a snort and climbed into the passenger seat. The Alfa tore out even before I'd shut the door. It turned at the end of the street, tires screeching, and we could see an empty crossroad twenty meters in front of us, a red traffic light, but no 504. Haymann went three meters past the light and we looked in every direction, but there was nothing.

"Great job tailing them," I remarked.

"It's your fault. You're always arguing!"

"It doesn't matter. Let's step on it. Head for Pont de Neuilly."

"Yes, boss."

Haymann started the car again. We turned onto boulevard Malesherbes and headed northwest.

"Say, Charlotte. Renée Mouzon got to Rose's office after you did, right?" I asked.

"No, she got there before me. She got to the building after I did, but by the time I'd finished explaining why I was there and managed to see the big boss, she was just hanging up her shitty raincoat."

"So," I said, "she didn't go to work this morning. She woke up with a terrible hangover, she was worried about Lionel, and maybe she spent the morning trying to reach him."

"Darling Lionel," said Charlotte calmly.

"Maybe she even went to see him at Fontainebleau, maybe she *did* see him. He's not being held. You can't arrest people because they were shot with a hunting gun in a forest. In other words, when she arrived at the foundation around three fifteen, let's suppose that was the first time she'd seen her boss that day. She's depressed, almost in tears, her boss asks her to tell him what's wrong as soon as he's finished with Charlotte. She breaks down and tells him everything, including my stopping by yesterday. And what happens next? Kasper arrives and the two of them snatch Renée Mouzon. That's their reaction."

We were heading toward Neuilly by boulevard de Courcelles and avenue des Ternes, speeding excessively. The Alfa was vibrating.

"That's nothing but supposition," declared Haymann bookishly.

"Not at all! It's four thirty. Between three thirty and four, Rose had just enough time to listen to his secretary's story and call Kasper."

"Whoa!" said Charlotte. "You think they're going to gun her down?"

"No," replied Haymann. "They're oafs, but not to that extent. They'll just take her out of circulation."

"To the countryside," I said.

Charlotte squinted at the two of us suspiciously.

"Yeah, okay," she said slowly. "They'll take her to the countryside. So can you tell me why we're rushing toward Neuilly instead of toward Meaux?"

Haymann and I thought about the question for ten seconds or so. Then Haymann braked violently and jerked the Alfa alongside a sidewalk. Through the windshield he pointed to a bookstore.

"Since you're such a clever one," he said to Charlotte, "go buy us a Michelin map."

Charlotte chuckled insultingly and went to buy the map. I sat in silence next to Haymann for a moment.

"Damn!" I shouted next. "I saw them pick her up. I thought they'd stop by her place in Neuilly to grab a suitcase with some of her personal things and that we'd have the chance to find them and follow them. Damn! It was a good idea, really!"

"Of course it was, Eugène. No one's criticizing you," said Haymann. He glared straight ahead through the windshield. "The thing is," he stated, "they're more intelligent than we are. It's sickening."

When Charlotte came back with the Michelin map "150 Kilometers Around Paris," we drove off, got on the ring road, then went through the Paris suburbs toward Meaux. We were hardly driving fast, but behind us there was a blue cloud of burned oil. We kept our eyes on the cars that passed us. On the one hand, I would've been relieved to see the 504 with Renée Mouzon inside; I would've been relieved to see they hadn't simply taken the lady to some quiet spot to dump her body. On the other hand, I had no desire to find myself side by side with Cedric Kasper.

Whatever the case, the 504 didn't pass us. We had some trouble with the carburetor that slowed us down, and night was falling when, just past Meaux, we drove onto the main street of a small hick town called Doutremart. The town was built in the shape of a Y on the turnoff of a county road, and almost every other building was a farmhouse with a barnyard. As far as we could tell in the falling darkness, the region was hilly and wooded with not only quite a bit of grassland but also loam where corn and beets were growing. I rolled down my window and breathed in the night air.

"Shut that," said Haymann. "It stinks of cow manure."

"It stinks of pig shit," I said to correct him, rolling my window back up. "There's a difference."

"I don't give a fart about the difference," declared Haymann haughtily. "I despise the countryside, cows, pigs, and farmers."

On one of the branches of the Y where we were now driving, there were fewer farms and more ugly weekend homes. Suddenly the town came to an end and Haymann braked and pulled off to the side. The road in front of us climbed up and seemed to veer to the right. On our left, there was a hill, hard to make out in the dark, and a sort of big building on top of the hill, like a fortified farmhouse filled with narrow lights, sitting among several trees about eight hundred to a thousand meters away.

"Well, here we are," I said.

"Shall we attack?" asked Haymann with a worrisome cackle.

"First we try going in gently. Let's go back to the center of town, okay?"

We went back to the center of town. As we were once again driving along the main street, we were blinded by powerful headlights, and the 504 sped by us with a high-pitched sound.

"Bastard," groaned Haymann.

He stopped the Alfa along the sidewalk. Charlotte and I, turning around, saw the brake lights of the 504 disappear in the direction of the fortified farmhouse.

"Could you see if the woman was inside?" I asked.

"I could almost swear to it," said Charlotte.

"On top of everything else, she's got good eyesight," said Haymann.

About thirty meters in front of us we saw a lighted café and general store. It seemed to be the only shop around. We got out of the car and walked over to the shop. It was hot inside. The floor was tiled, the countertop was made of real zinc that the Germans hadn't managed to steal, and the walls were decorated with garish four-color photos of aggressive-looking soccer teams. In the back room, a dozen or so farmers of all ages (no women) were staring at a black-and-white TV showing a grayish film.

"What the heck is that?" Charlotte mumbled, leaning forward.

"That's Pierre Richard-Willm," Haymann said. "You're too young to know who he is."

"Oh, right, it's Feyder's *Le grand jeu*," said Charlotte, and Haymann looked at her out of the corner of his eye.

In the meantime, the manager—a tall fat guy with frizzy hair, a snub nose, and a big apron over his vast belly, drew himself away from a tableful of people in the back room, slid behind the counter, and asked what he could serve us. Haymann and the girl ordered grogs and I ordered a coffee and asked if I could make a phone call. The fat man pointed to a phone on the counter and went over to his percolator. I made my call.

"Community of Reformed Skoptsy. May I help you?"

It was the same voice as last time.

"Good evening, miss," I said. "I'm calling to get some information about a stay with you."

"Yes, sir. Do you have a sign-up number?"

"No. I simply heard about your institute, and I heard only good things. Do I need to sign up in advance?"

"You have to fill out some forms, sir. You need to call on our Paris office." (She gave me an address.)

"That's difficult," I said. "I have a very busy schedule. I'm an entrepreneur, see?"

"Yes, sir." (She couldn't give a damn.)

"I just managed to free up my calendar unexpectedly for a few days, and I would have wanted to come right away, tomorrow or even today if that were possible."

"I'm terribly sorry, sir" (she was lying, she didn't give a flying fuck) "but you must fill out some forms. In any case, we're full at the moment. So sorry. Peace be with you, sir."

"You too," I grumbled, but she'd already hung up. I placed my finger on the lever and requested another number, but there was no answer: Coccioli wasn't home.

I went back to Charlotte and Haymann, who had ordered plates of charcuterie and bread.

"So?" asked Haymann.

I didn't answer. I sat down with them and mechanically began eating huge chunks of bread. I took out a ballpoint pen, grabbed Charlotte's paper napkin, and scribbled a kind of flowchart that looked something like this:

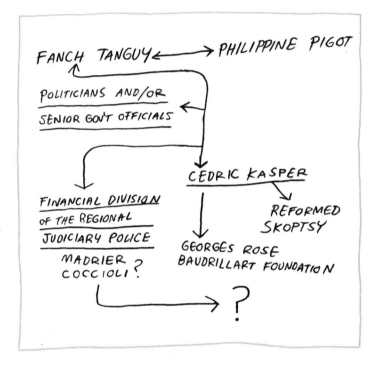

I could have added a few names: Renée Mouzon, Marthe Pigot, Charles Pradier, and so on, and even more arrows indicating relationships, but that wouldn't have made the flowchart any clearer, and it already wasn't clear at all. The only thing vaguely interesting on it was the big question mark at the bottom.

"What might the financial division of the Marseilles

regional police have discovered?" I wrote below the question mark, and then skipped a space. I sucked on the tip of my ballpoint and wrote: "What the fuck are all these people up to?" And I added three arrows connecting Tanguy, the Baudrillart Foundation, and the Skoptsy to the big final question mark. Charlotte was looking over my shoulder at the flowchart, which had become illegible. But there's only one possible answer, I said to myself, even though there are two questions. And as my gaze was wandering over toward the back room, I absent-mindedly noticed an old farmer with a completely bald head. And I suddenly remembered where I'd seen the driver of the 504.

"Jesus Christ!" I said.

I raised my arm to call over the waiter. He reluctantly tore his eyes from *Le grand jeu*.

"Can I get you something else, lady and gentlemen?"

"No," I said. "But I'd like to ask you a question."

"I know what it is," said Charlotte.

"Don't be ridiculous."

"I'll bet you ten thousand."

"You're kidding, right?" asked the waiter.

"No, I'd really like to ask you a question—"

"Yes," said Charlotte calmly. "Besides the manure, isn't there something else in this charming village that stinks?"

13

"GREAT, perfect, excellent!" roared Haymann from the backseat. "Don't bother explaining anything to me, but at least get that wisenheimer to stop her sniggering. It's exasperating!"

We were driving to Paris at night. I was at the wheel. And it's true that Charlotte, sitting next to me, was sniggering annoyingly.

"I'm sniggering," she said, "because I find the face Tarpon is making to be very amusing."

"I'm not making a face."

"Oh yes you are! You're angry, very angry. Darling Eugène, you're not the only one capable of guessing what's going on."

"Guessing!" I repeated furiously.

"It wasn't that complicated in any case. I won't even ask for my ten thousand francs."

"Oh yes you will!" I said. "I'll give them to you, all right!"

"Don't bother. You didn't stick to the bet."

"Are you two gonna stop fooling around?" asked Haymann. "What are you talking about?"

"We're talking about the ten-thousand-franc question," said Charlotte. "And the question is: What stinks?"

"Go ahead," I said. "Be a showoff."

"And the answer . . . the answer is not at all 'the billy goat,' contrary to what generations of unruly schoolboys told generations of bearded supervisors. The answer is: the Reformed Skoptsy. They're the ones who stink. Or, to repeat the words of the kindly peasant barman, 'the whole gang of Parisians and priests back there.'"

"I've had it. I'm getting out of this car," Haymann stated.

"Incense, incense burners, aromatic logs, saunas, sulfur baths," said Charlotte. "There's no question that the Community of Reformed Skoptsy stinks to high heaven. And add in acetone, acetic anhydride, hydrochloric acid, and tartaric acid, and we've got ourselves a typical case of perfect pollution. I'd be curious to see their water bill, but of course with all those baths, it's perfectly camouflaged." (She turned toward the backseat.) "Haymann, dear," she said, "the products I'm talking about allow one, through a difficult and dangerous process, to convert morphine into heroin."

We got off at Meaux. I turned on the windshield wipers because it had started to rain. I noticed the blades were ratty and practically useless.

"Well, well," said Haymann dreamily after a long pause. "Your knowledge of chemistry is excellent."

"I have a degree. But bear in mind, Haymann dear, that the great detective Eugène Tarpon and I are at the moment barking up the wrong tree. Several kilometers from the right tree. The only elements that have guided our stupendous intuition are: Number one, the roots of all this go back to Marseilles, and Madrier, God rest his soul, stumbled across those roots. And two, a pseudo-religious community has the possibility of emitting a great mass of mephitic vapors without frightening the peasants. It is possible, though, that the Reformed Skoptsy only stink of incense. Why are you snickering, Tarpon? You know that there's a fifty percent chance we're wrong."

"You really only drew your conclusions from those two elements and nothing else?" I asked.

"You should drive more slowly, we can't see a thing," Charlotte remarked. "Is my logic missing something?"

"Nothing you were supposed to know. See," I said, "before this unbelievable shitstorm hit me, I was on an ordinary little job, working for a pharmacist who suspects his employees of stealing from the till."

I told them about Mr. Jude's problems, and how I'd followed one Albert Pérez to Dieppe, and how he'd won big at chemin de fer, against an American.

"Of course, I figured it was Albert Pérez who was stealing from Jude. I discounted the fact that he'd won that night. I instinctively supposed he'd lost on previous nights. I thought he'd just had a stroke of luck. But I was totally off base. There were two guys at the table winning shitloads from the American. One was Albert Pérez and the other guy had a shiny bald pate. He's the driver of the 504."

"Oh, God! I see!" Haymann said.

"Now I'm the one who's lost," Charlotte said.

"Those guys aren't gamblers. They're money launderers."

"I'm still lost."

"You don't need to explain to the cops or the tax men or anyone where money you won gambling comes from because it was won in front of witnesses. The American in Dieppe was purposefully losing to Pérez and the driver. He wasn't gambling with them. He was paying them a huge amount."

Charlotte was contemplating what I'd just said. So was I. Something was bugging me, and once again she beat me to it.

"Hey!" she cried. "It's mindboggling."

"What's mindboggling?"

"Well, you're on the trail of this bullshit Skoptsy community, and meanwhile they're making drugs and they have people laundering money for them in certain circles and stuff like that. And then just by chance, a few days before the shitstorm starts, you run into one of their launderers? You've gotta admit, it's mindboggling."

"It's mindboggling. Or else," I said, "it wasn't by chance."

We got back to Paris at about 10:00 p.m. At 10:15 we had parked near Jules's apartment and climbed upstairs. At 10:17 I called the home of good old Mr. Jude. I didn't think I'd get the information I wanted, seeing as how in Jude's eyes, honest pharmacist that he was, I was no more than a jailbird being pursued by the law.

"Where'd you disappear to?" Mr. Jude exclaimed. "I called your place at least ten times but there was no answer."

"Don't you read the papers?"

"Just the sports section. Why?"

"No reason. Don't worry, I'm on the right track. I just wanted to know if you've done anything since Sunday. Called the police, for example, or spoken to Albert Pérez?"

"Well, I should have! Don't you know that the little bastard has disappeared?"

"Of course," I lied reflexively, because Mr. Jude was my client. I didn't have any others, and I had a bill of some three thousand francs to submit to him—the only income I had in sight—if this whole business would just calm down. "Of course," I repeated. "But don't worry. He's not the one stealing from you."

"Not the one?"

"He doesn't need to. I don't have time to fill you in, but I'm sure of it. How did you know he'd split?"

"How? Uh, well, he didn't come to work on Monday

afternoon, so I tried to get him on the phone but he didn't answer. And yesterday I went to his place but there was no one there and the shutters were closed. Obviously, he's disappeared somewhere."

"Okay, thanks. Don't worry," I repeated for the third or fourth time. "I'll have the results for you in a few days. I'll keep you posted."

"Wait just a sec there!" Mr. Jude shouted, and I hung up.

Haymann and Charlotte were absorbed in a game of Chinese chess. I observed them for a moment. All the pieces were identically shaped. Only the ideograms painted on them were different. I didn't understand the ideograms and I didn't understand their placement. The two players didn't see me slip out of the living room and they didn't hear me leave the apartment.

I parked the car on rue Championnet near a crosswalk. I went up to Albert Pérez's apartment. There was no list of residents in the hallway, but I had the lab technician's exact address, including the number of his apartment on the attic floor of a bourgeois and well-maintained building.

When I got to his door, I undid the safety catch on the Czech pistol. I was about to knock when I noticed a small space of two or three centimeters between the door and the doorframe. I pushed the door open with the tip of my foot.

I saw a maid's room with a sink in one corner and a hot plate in another. As for furniture, there was space only for a wardrobe, two chairs, and a big bed. The room was in complete disorder, with dirty socks and shirts on the floor and two ties hanging from the window handle. The shutters were closed. It wasn't the sort of disorder left behind after a search.

Above the bed was a large plasticized poster of a naked Ursula Andress. Albert Pérez was sitting, his back to the wall, at Ursula's feet, next to a lighted bedside lamp with a red lampshade. He had black holes in his chest and a bunch of blood blobs on his stomach. He'd been dead for some time because he was starting to smell and several flies buzzed around in the room, even though we were in the middle of November.

I did a quick search of the place, being careful not to leave any fingerprints. On the floor I found two empty shell casings on which I could read SUPER-X and 45 AUTO. In the wardrobe I found clothes and fifteen one-hundred-franc bills in a cardboard box, along with some papers like we all have— old love letters, a photograph of an elderly couple on a front stairway, and a military service record. I pocketed the money. I left.

When I got back to Jules's apartment, Charlotte and Haymann were still playing Chinese chess. I don't think they even noticed my absence. I picked up the phone book that lists people by their address, found the listing for the residents of Square Saint-Lambert, and scrutinized it. I found the address I was looking for.

"Checkmate," said Charlotte.

"Little bitch," Haymann replied.

I looked at the board. I still didn't understand the placement of the pieces. Haymann raised his head toward me.

"I think that's the end," said Haymann. "I want to take her cannon with my elephant, or her chariot with my officer, but I can't take both at the same time. You're very pale, Tarpon. You okay?"

"Just a bit tired," I said, then pointed to the chessboard. "But if you take this thing with that thing," I added, "aren't you covered?"

"No. Because the cannon gives check by jumping over the

officer. It's the opposite of discovered check, Tarpon. That's the way the cannon works, with something in its way."

"Yeah," I said. "Just like me with Officer Coccioli. Guess I was in his way."

"Where are you going?" Charlotte asked, but I was already on the landing.

I remained for a good while in the Alfa on Square Saint-Lambert looking at the entrance to Coccioli's building and the whole neighborhood. It seemed as if the cop wasn't being tailed anymore because I didn't see another soul. I went into the building. Coccioli's name was inserted in some little transparent plastic thingy above a doorbell on the ground floor. I rang forcefully.

Coccioli opened the door. He was in his shirtsleeves, the sleeves rolled up on his hairless biceps, his tie loosened, his hair slightly disheveled.

"Just in time," he said.

I shoved him back with the palm of my hand and entered the apartment. I closed the door behind me with my heel.

"Now, now, Tarpon. Let's not get agitated," he said.

I grabbed him by the tie and threw him in the other direction toward the opposite wall. The back of his head hit the plaster with a hollow sound and Coccioli fell to the floor with a grimace. He stayed sitting there, massaging his head. I took the Czech 7.62 from my pocket and cocked it.

"You're gonna tell me about Albert Pérez," I ordered. "And the rest. I don't have much left to lose. I'll shoot you right now."

"No you won't," said Coccioli fawningly. "You're not gonna shoot me."

"For God's sake!" I shouted. (Not because I was on edge but because from time to time it does a body good.)

"That's enough," said Coccioli, less fawningly. "Calm down. Albert Pérez is my informant, if you want to know. He's home on rue Championnet and he's dead. I assume you know that. They probably did him on Sunday or Monday morning. Put your gun down."

"Yes, Tarpon, put it down," advised Commissioner Chauffard who had opened the door to the living room behind my back and was pointing an S&W Terrier revolver at me.

14

UNDER normal circumstances, you've got to take seriously someone who's aiming a gun at you. But on this occasion, I giggled; I must have been slightly wound up. With my left hand I grabbed the Terrier away from Chauffard and with my right I slammed him in the face with the side of the 7.62.

"Tarpon, come on! I mean, Christ," said Coccioli while Chauffard was wobbling backward in the living room. He wound up falling on his ass and moaning; he brought his fingers to his face where drops of blood were dribbling down.

I followed Chauffard into the living room. I was holding the 7.62 properly and the Terrier by the barrel. My lower lip was trembling, my left eyelid contracting spasmodically. Chauffard remained seated on the carpet and sniffled miserably into his toothbrush mustache. There was a third guy in the room in his shirtsleeves. He was in his forties, smallish, with a wide, long torso and too-short legs. He had a baby face and gray hair like steel wool. He had an empty holster on his right shoulder and in his right hand he held a Terrier identical to the one I was holding by the barrel. He wasn't aiming it at me. I walked toward him. He placed his revolver on the table and sat down in a chair. I felt like whacking him on the head with the gun, but he was looking at me calmly and seemed vaguely heartbroken. On the table sat a porcelain soup bowl atop a porcelain plate. I tossed my two guns on the floor. I grabbed the soup bowl, which was empty and dusty, and I slammed it down on the plate. Everything broke into big pieces.

"Oh, shit, not my Moustier porcelain!" wailed Coccioli as he walked into the room.

I turned toward him with the intention of carrying out more violence, but he immediately sat down in a chair.

"Finished with your hysterics?" asked the man with the steel-wool hair as Coccioli shouted at me, "You're a pig, Tarpon. Those were old Moustiers, a family souvenir worth a fortune. You disappoint me."

"Oh? And what about you?" I asked calmly. "You don't think you're a pig? Huh?" (I raised my arm and pressed two fingers against the corner of my left eyelid. The spasmodic contraction ceased.)

"I did what was for the best," said Coccioli. "You came and sowed chaos in a very delicate affair, one I didn't have under control. All of us here have our careers on the line, if not our lives."

"Why don't you explain it, then. I don't want to ask you any questions because I may wind up getting really furious. I'll just listen."

"With pleasure," Coccioli declared irrationally, and I sat down at the table. I bumped into the knee of the guy with the steel-wool hair; he nodded at me smugly.

"Commissioner Grazzelloni. Drug squad."

"Charmed..."

"Same here."

"...I'm sure!" I shouted.

"Albert Pérez was my informant," Coccioli said again, resting his elbows on the table. "I'd nabbed him about two years ago for a small infraction; it doesn't matter, it's not related. A real customer, that Pérez. By day an honest pharmaceutical assistant, by night a petty criminal, the kind of creep who likes to hang out in the Montmartre bars to rub elbows with thugs, do them small favors, become friendly with them. You see the type. Being an informant for the cops probably excited him even more. A shady sort. An intellectual. May he rest in peace."

Chauffard had stood up. He had a cut on his cheek and a little blood was still trickling from his nostril. He went to look in a gilt-framed mirror and palpated his nose with displeasure. Then he walked back toward us and cast a hostile glance my way. He sat down at the table, grabbed an open pack of small bottles of Kronenbourg, and gestured to offer us one. I nodded. He uncapped a bottle with his bare hand and passed it to me. I sipped.

Meanwhile Coccioli continued his story. Five or six months earlier, a couple of Pérez's shifty friends knew he liked to gamble so they offered him a way to earn his living gambling: by laundering money in Parisian circles and nearby casinos, mostly in Normandy. He'd accepted without even asking Coccioli's opinion.

"I wrote up a little report on principle," said the cop, "without mentioning my source, and I followed the affair in my spare time. I didn't know where it would lead. I never thought it would turn out to be important, because Pérez was a pathetic little guy. Except that after three months something like fifty million old francs had passed through his hands. And sometimes there was another guy who raked it in at the same time as Pérez. And maybe there were other guys, too. Around five or six. Multiply fifty million by five or six and you don't have a minor business to deal with."

"Is it the Americans who are paying?"

"Mostly, yes. Germans too. And once or twice, Italians."

"Did you manage to figure out where the money was coming from?"

"I wrote reports," said Coccioli, looking world-weary. "He dropped it off every Monday morning in a café near Saint-Augustin. It would have been tough to find out more. I didn't want to interrogate the café worker because I didn't know if he was keeping the briefcase for someone else or if he himself was the next link in the chain. I could have asked for the café to be watched using a dozen different cops but in the end it was my affair, and I wanted to go as far as I could on my own, like a big boy."

"Still—" I said.

"Still nothing," Chauffard cut in. "It's lucky Coccioli continued on his own. If he'd asked for backup, the affair would have been taken away from him and everything would have stopped there."

"I doubt it."

"Well, you shouldn't," Coccioli said dryly. "Because as soon as I'd gone up the ranks I was stopped in my tracks. It took me three weeks to identify the guy who carried the briefcase out of the bistro. Decent-looking guy, bourgeois, Legion of Honor, and so on. He'd come drink his coffee there every weekday before going back to his office."

"The Stanislas Baudrillart Foundation," I said.

Coccioli glanced at me. "Yeah. The guy was Georges Rose, the foundation boss."

"I know."

Coccioli uncapped his beer with a bottle opener. "Once we got to him, it was out of my hands. I drew up another report, but this one was very forceful."

I nodded. I understood. "Very forceful" for Coccioli meant that there were lots of exclamation marks.

"Forty-eight hours later," the officer said, "Commissioner Madrier 'ran into' me. He'd seen my report, which is not normal. It should never have wound up in his hands, at least not so quickly. He told me to drop the case."

"Just like that?"

"Oh, well, he said stuff that made sense, for example, that I was encroaching on his territory. He personally already had his eye on the foundation. But this business had a ton of ramifications that I couldn't understand so the best thing for me to do would be to fuck off and let him carry out his investigation in peace, in his own time, and so on and so forth."

Coccioli sighed, grabbed his beer and emptied three-quarters of the small bottle, which made a slapping sound on the table when his arm fell. Foam had formed, rising to the neck.

"And incidentally," I said, "Madrier wanted to know your source."

"Yeah, incidentally. I refused."

"That must have made him happy."

"He seemed to take it very well. You know, refusing to share informants, even among friends, is not considered impolite."

"Impolite," I repeated. "Now there's a word I like in this context. And then? Is that when I miraculously appear?"

"No, not quite yet. First, Philippine Pigot disappears."

"Huh?" I said.

"I swear on my mother's head! It was sheer chance! Marthe Pigot had a sister in the provinces who knows my aunt. Obviously I didn't know about the existence of this sister, or Marthe Pigot, or Philippine. But our boys have a huge organization, a part of which exists to handle a shitload of dough. So they could comb through every single one of their employees, create files on them, and so on. There was a link, indirect as it was, between Philippine Pigot and me. They learned from Madrier that I had a mole in their group. Bye-bye Philippine. I suppose we'll find her body one of these days."

Now it was my turn to grab my little beer bottle. I downed it in one gulp and let out a big, open-mouthed sigh, wiping the foam mustache from my mouth. Chauffard mechanically uncapped another Kronenbourg and set it down in front of me.

"Thanks," I said to Chauffard; and to Coccioli: "What about Fanch Tanguy in this mess?"

Coccioli shrugged.

"Most likely," said Grazzelloni (his voice was calm and warm, and beautifully resonant, which clashed with his physique) "most likely there is no relationship whatsoever. Fanch Tanguy was a French gestapo who was assassinated for one reason or another by a Maquis in 1944. Old Lady Pigot, for one reason or another, imagined he was still alive somewhere and that he was the one who'd kidnapped Philippine. Something she'd dreamed up. False trail, Tarpon."

"Marthe Pigot was shot because she mentioned Fanch Tanguy."

"She was shot because she was Philippine's mother and they thought she might know too much about the Baudrillart Foundation. End of story."

"Okay, sure," I said, turning toward Coccioli. "What happens next? I have a feeling that I'll find it even more interesting."

"What happens next is that in the middle of all this mess, you started to tail Pérez. Not only did he spot you but another of his colleagues—I mean another money collector—spotted you as well."

"While you're at it, say how clumsy I am, why don't you."

"It's impossible to tail someone in the car when you're alone," declared Chauffard pointedly. "It's just plain stupid to try."

"You were tailing him for his boss, I presume?" Coccioli said. "There's a girl stealing from the register at the pharmacy. Pérez mentioned it to me in passing. A Huguette something or other."

"Ah. I see," I said.

"Anyway," said Coccioli, "it's a pain in the ass. And at the same time, Old Lady Pigot was on my back. So I got an idea all of a sudden."

"You piece of shit," I commented.

"I wanted to keep on the affair, discreetly. Then all of a sudden, I thought that maybe I shouldn't be discreet! Maybe it would be better to send a guy with drums and trumpets and bayonet at the ready, a guy who could make all those blackhearted bastards shake in their boots. Obviously, I had to remain undercover. But if I got you involved . . ."

"Fantastic," I said. "Genius. By accident I start to tail two money launderers for a big mob. I know nothing about them. The same big mob just made a chick disappear, and probably killed her, and you involve me directly in the chick's disappearance, and I still know nothing about anything. Do you know what I would've done in their shoes?"

"Uh . . ."

"I would have exterminated me," I stammered. "I would have exterminated Eugène Tarpon immediately, quickly. I wouldn't even have waited as long as they did." (The spasmodic contraction suddenly resurfaced on my left eyelid. I stood up, knocking over my chair.) "Christ!" I said, almost softly. "Try to tell me to my face that you didn't think that was a possibility."

"Well, uh, of course," said Coccioli, "there was a risk. I made you do something risky. I understand why you're angry."

I walked across the living room. There were tons of old Moustiers in a glass-door sideboard.

"Evil little bastard," I said. "I'm not afraid of risk. Can you understand that?"

I didn't go into details. I grabbed the sideboard and tipped it forward. Coccioli let out a shrill exclamation. The sideboard fell on the corner of the table. It gives me great pleasure to say that both the sideboard and the table broke. The corner of the table snapped clean off, one side of the sideboard cracked, and all the glass panes fell down in a rain of dishware—platters, dishes, cups, saucers, teapots, bowls, gravy boats, mustard pots shattered on the floor in a great racket.

"You're out of your mind, Tarpon! Do something, for God's sake!" Coccioli shouted at the two others who hadn't budged.

"The damage is already done," Chauffard replied.

"In this sort of business, my dear Coccioli," said Grazzelloni, "you know something always has to be sacrificed."

I went to sit back down at what was left of the table. I made eye contact with Chauffard and it seemed to me he was slightly amused and even slightly approving.

"I feel better," I remarked.

"You just destroyed something like eight hundred thousand old francs worth of porcelain," Coccioli declared bitterly.

"Coccioli," said Grazzelloni, "don't be so gloomy."

"What is all this?" I asked, looking from one commissioner to the other. "A meeting of honest cops? There are only three of you," I commented.

"You've earned the right to sneer," Grazzelloni said, sighing.

"One doesn't need to earn the right to sneer," I replied dramatically. "But I wasn't sneering. There are only three of you. Couldn't there be fifteen or twenty?"

"If it's just for a meeting…"

"It's for leaving your jurisdiction and doing a search without a warrant. It's to destroy this fucking mafia! It's to massacre their lab and grab five or six bastards, or maybe twelve, I have no idea, and to make them give evidence by whacking them on the ass with a gun and to destroy everything, so there!" (I stopped to catch my breath.) "Happy?" I asked.

"Do you know where their lab is?"

"Do you have fifteen or twenty guys, yes or no?"

"We should be able to get fifteen," Chauffard said.

"And then," I said, "you're going to have to obey me a little, because it's a long shot."

I explained what I knew. They'd never heard of the Community of Reformed Skoptsy and they were interested. Nonetheless, after six or seven sentences, they started shouting and interrupting me, declaring the danger and the pointlessness of my plans. In their opinion, we only needed to raid the Skoptsy.

"Oh, yeah, great," I said. "And why don't you just get a search warrant while you're at it."

"No can do. Their walls have ears."

"And if you find them without a warrant and they've moved their lab, how'll that make you look? What will happen to your precious careers? And them? They'll be home free for how long afterward?"

"True enough," Chauffard said.

I looked at him. Of the three of them, he was the one who inspired the least mistrust in me. Coccioli was a double-crossing SOB, mostly worried about holding on to power. There was something too civilized about Grazzelloni, too polished, worldly almost. He was a man who liked smoothing things over and dividing them up. But Chauffard, with his chubbiness, his toothbrush mustache, his pipe, and his limited vocabulary, was a peasant like me. A long time ago I truly thought that being a cop was a good thing, in order to promote justice and peace by getting rid of the bad guys. Looking at Chauffard, I remembered I used to believe that a long time ago.

"I'm with you," Chauffard said to me.

"Thank you."

"You're welcome."

"The first thing I'm going to ask you," I said, "is to lend me a hand for a break-in."

15

AND WE had a tedious, busy night.

First, in Chauffard's worn-out 404, we traveled to avenue Émile Deschanel, to the address the suave receptionist of the Reformed Skoptsy had given me over the phone, and we burgled the Parisian office of the sect. Coccioli sweated in fear.

There was a waiting room with magazines and reproductions of Fuseli paintings, and two offices, one that apparently served to receive visitors, the other buried in filing cabinets. The place was littered with brochures about yoga, saunas, how to be healthy with plants, and Sri Dugashvilli's, or some other fool's, true messages. And there were files on clients. There was one marked REJECTED CANDIDATES in which we found index cards that had been filled out by a doctor, two chemical engineers, and others. We couldn't immediately see the reasons the candidacies of the others had been rejected, but the chemists' and the doctor's rejections were obvious.

There was a larger file with index cards filled out by the accepted candidates. The information on these cards was very detailed: not only last name, first name, address, date of birth, and so on, but also work history, degrees, etc. And then height, weight, hair color, eye color; the only thing missing was their fingerprints. There was a checkbox in the top right-hand corner of each card with a handwritten note:

Arrival 11/16, or Arrival 11/18, or Arrival 11/19, etc. It was November 17 and those were the dates of arrival for the week, past and future. I checked to see if I could find an arrival for the next day—actually, for today, because it was 1:00 a.m.

"You're screwed," said Grazzelloni over my shoulder. "They're all couples."

"Well, shit," I said. "I'll bring a woman and I know exactly which one."

"If you come across that Kasper or anyone else who could recognize you, it would be very dangerous, you know. And you're talking about bringing a woman?"

"Fuck off," I murmured. I was furious. I don't know at whom.

After a while, we put everything back very carefully and we left the premises without a trace of having been there. We'd selected a single arrival for the following day, a couple from Versailles. We got to their place at 2:30 a.m.

We had to ring the bell for a long time to wake them up, and then we had to haggle at the door, and Chauffard had to slip his police ID under it for them to open it.

They'd been partying the night before. Their living room was chock-full of unemptied ashtrays, dirty glasses, and records that hadn't been put back in their jackets. The living-room table was covered with a tablecloth drowning in crumbs, ashes, and wine stains. They must have had at least ten grams of alcohol in their blood, so that the first problem we came up against was one of simple comprehension.

The second problem was financial. They had paid an advance of two thousand francs to the Community of Reformed Skoptsy for their stay. The cops with me had very little cash on them. To smooth things over, I had to give the couple the fifteen hundred francs I'd taken from Pérez's place, plus five hundred francs that were part of the booty I'd gotten by stealing from Kasper and the guy wearing just his shirt.

But even before all that, we'd come up against a more serious problem that could have proved unsolvable. Our little duckies were reluctant to collaborate with the police. They could have totally refused. This behavior is increasingly prevalent in every social class. I can't blame the social classes. As for our duckies—Monsieur and Madame Jacques Blondeau, to be precise—they held extreme right-wing views and their reluctance was of the most vulgar and reactionary kind, as could be seen by the presence on their table of *Minute*, a weekly magazine that was both vulgar and reactionary. For a time, the negotiations between my buddies and the Blondeau couple seemed at an impasse. But then I grabbed François Brigneau's dirty little magazine (there was wine spilled on it), that is, *Minute*. I stated that I was pleased to meet a couple who enjoyed Brigneau's publication. I claimed I did too. As I spoke, I waved Brigneau's little crumpled magazine around to lend support to my words. And in this way I created a climate of trust. I hinted that the secret mission my friends and I had been assigned had political connotations that would please a man who was pleased by the contents of Brigneau's magazine. Chauffard entered into my game and started calling me "Colonel." At last, when I'd set the pathetic, dirty, wrinkled magazine back on the edge of the table, and when we'd left the Blondeaus' place, I had in my pocket two little moleskin card holders that Monsieur Blondeau had given me containing various pamphlets about the Community of Reformed Skoptsy, along with two tickets in the names of Monsieur and Madame Blondeau, and two badges. And we had Monsieur and Madame's promise that they would keep silent about our visit.

"Do you really think they'll keep quiet?" Chauffard asked me as we headed toward Paris.

"They'll talk about it for a minute," I said. "Then they'll go to bed. And even if they were to tell someone in the end, it wouldn't be before tomorrow in the middle or at the end of the day. At worst, they'll tell their friends but not a lawyer or the police. At least not yet. And definitely not the Reformed Skoptsy. By the time it surfaces, let's hope everything will be over. You need to be there in twelve hours, by the way."

"With fifteen men?"

"Twenty would be better."

"We'll do the best we can, Tarpon. For now, we all need to get some sleep."

I agreed. Approximately one hour later when I'd straightened out all the final details with Chauffard, I went back to Jules's place. I wanted desperately just to lie down on the carpet in the entranceway. The light was on in the living room. I went in. Haymann was sitting on the sofa and pouring himself a glass of Spanish cognac. Charlotte, on all fours in front of the record player, was putting on an album.

"You oughta be in bed," I said. "We've got a rough day coming."

"Yeah, right," said Charlotte as she stood up. "We should be in bed tossing and turning, wondering what happened to you."

"A woman in love," mumbled Haymann, and Charlotte called him a jerk.

"And what's *this* racket?" I asked, and Charlotte told me it was Cecil Taylor.

"And this other moron," she said, waving her arm toward Haymann, "this other moron disappeared for two hours and came back drunk as a skunk."

"There wasn't a drop to drink in this house," Haymann sighed. "We'd gone through all of Jules's stock. And at midnight, the stores are closed. As a result, I had to appeal to some friends. He's from Brittany, because he's Spanish," he added, completely incomprehensibly, as he poured himself another little drink, and he looked at me clear-eyed.

"Does the name Professor Bachhauffer, Bachhauffer with two *h*'s, mean anything to you?" he asked.

I shook my head, threw the sheepskin jacket in a corner of the room, and took off my shoes without bothering to untie them, for which my mom always scolded me. I started to unbutton my shirt.

"Hey there!" cried Charlotte. "You're not going to strip naked, are you?"

"Did Melis-Sanz call Toulouse or something?" I asked Haymann.

"Your deductive reasoning skills are improving."

"Professor Bachhauffer with two *h*'s," I said. "I suppose he's the guy who was in the car with Fanch Tanguy, and who was nabbed by the Corps Francs, and who escaped. So, since you know everything about the Collaboration, who is Professor Bachhauffer?"

"No idea," said Haymann, shrugging. "Never heard the name."

"Get off my bed," I ordered Haymann, who got off, taking his glass with him. I slipped out of my trousers, rolled myself up in the blanket, and stretched out on the sofa.

"Find an alarm clock," I said, "and set it. We need to get up in four hours."

And I must have fallen asleep in the middle of a sentence because I didn't feel at all rested but it was light outside, it was 10:00 a.m., the morning of November 18. I met Haymann and Charlotte in the kitchen. While we were drinking the coffee Charlotte had made, I started to speak as if I had stopped only a moment before, saying, no, having thought about it, it wasn't possible to bring Charlotte. It was much too dangerous. And she told me to fuck off. And Coccioli arrived, badly shaven, with spare clips; and it took me a while to really wake up and then it was probably too late to change anyone's mind, we were already in the car on our way to Doutremart and the Community of Reformed Skoptsy, heading toward a bloodbath, a massacre, and deep shit.

16

AND THEN, well, everyone knows what happened next: the raid in the early hours between Thursday and Friday, the blood spilled, the lab stormed, the arrests, the network dismantled, the fallout, and how Georges Rose, former election official, compromised Deputy Mauchemps; and how Mauchemps grabbed on to his parliamentary immunity with all his might. Of course, everyone knows that wasn't enough to save him, so now he's in the slammer, although his poor health, or something or other, has allowed him to have a special diet. But maybe it'd be better if I told the story in chronological order.

Thursday after lunch at around 3:00, Charlotte and I arrived at the Community of Reformed Skoptsy. It took us a while to prepare. ("You really look like a cop," said Charlotte. "You need to look more like an exhausted executive.") I'd borrowed from Jules's closet a wine-colored corduroy suit, a flowered shirt, and ankle boots with four- or five-centimeter heels, which made me feel like I was wearing stilts. And Charlotte had "gently combed my hair," as she put it, which meant that she'd ruthlessly combed all my hair forward onto my forehead. And I had a Band-Aid on my nose.

"I look ridiculous," I remarked.

"As you should!" Charlotte replied. And since I asked if

all of that was really necessary, she'd shouted, "Obviously! If Kasper sees you from even three meters away, he'll recognize you. But maybe it'll be fifteen seconds too late. Put your hands in your pockets."

"That'll ruin the look."

"If Kasper's car is still there," said Coccioli, "you absolutely cannot go in. We'll figure something else out."

"Put your hands in your pockets, damn it! No, the trouser pockets. Belly forward. And smile! No, more stupidly. There. But keep going. Smile all the time."

"It stretches my mouth out."

"That's because your muscles aren't used to smiling. You never smile. And keep those hands in your pockets."

"Do you really think—"

"And call me 'sweetie'! We're a couple. And yes, I really think so. Every individual has a personality and it's that personality that has to be disguised."

"Now there's a truly literary idea."

"Just wait and see."

I saw. When we came across Kasper, he recognized us instantly from thirty meters away.

Before that, there was the drive there, then the visit, then the purification.

At the end of the drive, we watched the community's buildings through binoculars. We didn't see any suspicious activity. There were lots of cars in the back parking lots, but not the 504 from the previous night.

We returned to the village proper and left Haymann and Coccioli with the binoculars. I got behind the wheel of the Alfa, we left the village again, and drove back to the gates of the community.

Immediately, a seventeen- or eighteen-year-old monk of

some sort, with a shaved head and dirty feet, guided us to where we were to leave the Alfa in the parking lot. Most of the cars had Parisian plates.

Together the buildings looked like they belonged to a very big barnyard farm, with a few shed-like outbuildings. We were surrounded by woods and meadows where some slender-legged horses were grazing. The walls of the farmhouse were very thick, and the openings, high and narrow, were few. It was practically a fortified farm. Since the parking lot was in the back, we'd have to walk around half of the enclosure following the little monk until we reached the front door.

"If there are people trying to move their cars," I said to the little monk, "mine will be in the way."

"I know. We'll need your key."

I started to hand him my key. He backed away, closing his eyes.

"They'll take it at the front desk. I don't touch machines."

"My apologies."

"No need." (He opened his eyes and moved out in front of us again. He was barefoot. It was literally freezing out. The bottoms of his feet were covered with a thick layer of blackened callus.) "No need," he repeated. "You couldn't have known. You haven't been educated yet. But don't feel inferior. I'm the inferior, please believe me."

"As you wish," I assured him.

At the front door was a sort of booth with a kind of guard post, like you see at the entrances of military or government buildings. Inside the booth was a young, rather pretty brunette with curly hair and big blue nearsighted eyes. She wore a yellow acrylic smock with the little white collar of her blouse peeking out. At her request, we handed her our entrance tickets in the names of Monsieur and Madame Jacques

Blondeau and we put on our name tags with our assumed first names, that is, Jacques and Myriam. The brunette checked something off on a piece of paper attached to a board with a bulldog clip. Then we followed the young monk inside the property walls, and he gave us a tour.

Like I said, it was a barnyard farm, two stories, with its back to the northeast. In the body of the main building and its two wings, the upper level consisted only of bedrooms lining one continuous corridor. We were shown to our room. Its walls were whitewashed, like all the building's partition walls. We had a small window that let in a bit of light and looked northeast; we had a view of a wooded hillside, and under the window was the roof of a shed.

In the bedroom were two thick mats, a fair number of beige cushions, a wicker wardrobe, and nothing else. The young monk opened the wicker wardrobe; inside were blankets. We didn't have any luggage because the community wanted us to come baggage-free. Jacques and Myriam had already told me that, and it had been specified in the instructional brochure.

"It's pretty basic," I said, because the silence was weighing on me.

"It's inferior," said the little monk. "That's appropriate."

We went out of the room, leaving the door open. All along the corridor the doors to the rooms seemed to be open, and we could see the same deal in all of them: white walls, beige cushions, two mats, and a wicker wardrobe. That cost three hundred fifty francs a day per person and I could predict that the food would also be spartan, magnificently inferior—water and soy flour, for example.

I didn't have time to verify my predictions, however. As we were walking once again down the corridor, at the other end, about thirty meters away, I saw Kasper coming around the corner. I grabbed Charlotte by the elbow and turned sharply into the closest bedroom.

"What about here? And here? And here?" I asked nervously. "What's this?" (There were four people in the room, two men and two women, sitting on cushions. They looked at me questioningly and calmly. With one hand I held on to Charlotte. I'd slipped my other hand beneath my plum-colored jacket and my fingers brushed the grip of the Czech automatic, but I thought it was a bit too soon to open fire.)

"It's another bedroom," said the young monk, who had remained in the doorway.

"Welcome," said one of the seated men. "Are you new here?"

He didn't wait for my answer. He went back to doing the same thing as his companions, that is, tapping his knees with his palms very quickly while reciting words that sounded to me like Aranaranaranaranaranaranarana (but perhaps I misunderstood).

"Uh, let's move on," said the young monk, "or else we'll be late for the purification."

"Buddy," I whispered, "quite the opposite. We're going to be early."

At the same time I released the safety catch on the 7.62 and I stepped to the side so that I was back in the corridor. But the corridor was empty and Kasper was nowhere to be seen, as if it had been a dream. Yet I was sure I'd seen him, though I didn't think he'd seen us. And Charlotte kept glancing at me questioningly, slightly irritated because she found my behavior completely inexplicable.

"Okay," I said. "Let's move on."

We moved on. And I couldn't warn Charlotte in the presence of the young monk.

Following a young idiot monk when you expect to see a killer crop up at any moment causes a physical sensation that I highly recommend.

Some of the rooms were empty and others weren't. Some people were wearing beige robes and others were dressed in city clothes. Some were talking or reciting, others were doing absolutely nothing. I counted a dozen people, between thirty and fifty years old, as many men as women, all from what I suspected was a decent social class. Most of them seemed to take their presence here very seriously.

Later we learned that young monks and young nuns occupied the narrow building in front, with bedrooms upstairs and a sort of double gatehouse on each side of the main entrance. But our young monk didn't take us on a tour of this area. After the guests' bedrooms, he led us downstairs and showed us the inside of one wing, where there were workshops. Young monks, young nuns, beige robes, shaved heads, between seventeen and twenty-five years old were busy weaving fabrics, fabricating jewelry, baking bread, and turning bowls on a potter's wheel.

Obviously everywhere there were incense sticks and burners and the place reeked of incense and myrrh. Well, incense in any case, because I have no idea what myrrh smells like, I just said that to say it.

The place with the greatest mystical stench was in the southwest wing of the ground floor, in a weaving studio where you could see the entrance to a cellar blocked by an iron door with a security bar.

"And over there?" I asked the young monk, pointing.

"The cellar. Let's hurry along, please. There are two other people waiting so you can be purified all together."

We hurried along. On the ground floor of the main building were closed rooms and common halls, a cafeteria, a meeting room. At last we crossed a threshold and found ourselves in a tiled hall where a couple and a woman seemed to be waiting for us, and the young monk told us we'd arrived.

The couple consisted of a corpulent granny type wearing a mink coat, with platinum blond hair and an assertive bust, no doubt siliconed, and a pretty boy, ten years younger than the granny, also blond, with an ultraviolet tan. He was smoking a Celtique cigarette in a Dunhill cigarette holder.

"Welcome, Jacques and Myriam," the other woman said to us.

She wore a saffron-colored robe and a single-strand silver choker. Her head was shaved, and her eyebrows were totally plucked, which made her look like a staring bird. She held out four large plastic bags, one for each of us.

"Right now you are going to undress," she said out of the blue. "No doubt you would be more at ease if I told you first why it's necessary. But our goal is not to put you at ease, it is to debase you. In the outside world where material things have become all powerful, man does nothing without information. Here, material things are worthless, and it is the spirit that is all powerful. You will not get any information. You must simply submit. Joy does not come from information. Joy comes from debasement and discipline."

"Wait a sec!" growled the pretty boy, looking disgusted and yanking his cigarette holder from between his teeth.

"Silence!" the bird-eyed woman ordered.

The pretty boy seemed about to argue, but the woman in the mink glared at him and I distinctly saw her pinch his wrist. The pretty boy shrugged. The Buddhist nun, or whatever she was, had already turned away and was at the back of the room, where she opened a door. We were smacked in the face by waves of heat and noise.

In the room next door, which was huge, there was a pool about ten meters long and fifty centimeters deep, filled with warm water. Through the clouds of steam we could see some fifteen naked people in the pool, splashing and hollering and making friendly gestures toward us.

"Come one. Take off your close," said the nun with a hospitable smile.

"Take off your cloTHes," the pretty boy shouted.

"Excuse me?"

"CloTHes, not close!"

"Yes, well," said the nun batting her eyelids, "and put your things in the plastic bag. You'll get them back after the purification."

"Arabaranabanana!" shouted the bathers.

"This is bullshit! I told you it would be bullshit!" cried the pretty boy, turning toward his companion.

But she, seeming quite titillated, had taken off her mink coat and her skirt, and next she took off her blouse and exposed a structurally perfect bust, very large and apparently solid as a rock.

"Kasper is here," I whispered to Charlotte.

"Huh?"

"Kasper is around. I saw him. He didn't see us. A little while ago, upstairs."

"Are you sure?"

"Take off your cloTHes, take off your cloTHes!" the nun ordered us again, commandeering us like a schoolteacher lining up her pupils.

I directed my gaze to a point on the wall and I kept it

there as I undressed. I stuffed my clothes and my shoes into the plastic bag, carefully folding my jacket around the 7.62.

Through the steam, it was tough to tell if the gaze the singing bathers were directing at us was numinous or lecherous. Then the bald priestess collected our bags and the granny with the boob job was the first to rush toward the pool, giggling joyfully and bumping into me with one of her breasts. The pretty boy followed, glancing at me over his shoulder with a look somewhere between virility and moral collapse.

"Last one in . . ." I said to him and he instantly turned his head back around as he walked to the pool, bringing all his muscles into play.

When all of us had gotten into the pool up to our knees, we had to splash one another and chant like everyone else. At one moment it seemed to me that Charlotte was softly warbling banana, cabana, and "Hava Nagila" instead of arabaranabanana, but when I glanced at her, with her gorgeous eyes and her pretty breasts covered in droplets of water, she seemed as completely mystical as possible. Just then, a zealot placed his hand on her ass, and she lobbed him a good kick with her heel, without stopping her chanting.

All that lasted a while and felt to me like a good while longer. Finally, everyone left, except we four novices and the priestess who was cavorting and clapping poolside.

"Now," announced the bald woman, "I'm going to call you one at a time. First, Lucienne."

"That's me," the boob-jobbed granny said, rather absurdly.

She hauled herself up with a bit of difficulty. She was out of breath because she'd given all she had to the ceremony. She walked toward the exit door that the priestess indicated to her, opposite the one through which we had come in. Looking sickened, the pretty boy watched her disappear. We remained there for a few minutes not knowing what to do as the water lapped at our thighs. Then Charlotte was called. And five minutes later, I was called.

I was eager to get back the plastic bag, my clothes, and the 7.62. I went through the door and found myself in a small office. I closed the door behind me. There was another door on the other side of the room. My bag of clothes and a towel sat on a desk covered in brochures. I grabbed the towel. The door in front of me opened and Kasper walked in. His right arm was still in a cast and sling. With his left hand, he aimed a Walther PPK with white plastic grips at my navel.

"I knew this would happen," I remarked.

17

"GIVE me your weapon," I said next. "I'm grabbing two or three a day now. Soon I'm gonna be able to open up a gun-supply store."

He looked at me thoughtfully. "Get dressed."

"Allow me to dry myself first, please."

"Let's not waste any time, Tarpon, I'm on edge."

He said this in a very flat tone, which made his words sound absolutely astonishing, as if a yogurt you'd just started to eat suddenly screamed, "Hurry up! Finish me! I can't stand the pain of waiting!"

I pulled my clothes onto my damp skin. They didn't slide on easily. Stupidly, I searched for the 7.62, which was obviously no longer there.

"You're fucked and you know it," I said, fighting with the buttons on my flowered shirt. "I should hope you don't imagine I would have risked my life here, and with a woman on top of it, before we'd got you surrounded." (I closed the clasp of the gold watch on my wrist. It read 4:45. We'd agreed that Chauffard and Grazzelloni would arrive at the village at 6:30, with the fifteen or twenty cops they'd managed to recruit in the meantime. And I, or Charlotte, or both of us, sometime after 6:30, were supposed to disappear from the fake monastery and join our guys at the village snack bar in Doutremart, to let them know whether it was worth launching an attack, if they had a good chance of catching a bunch of bandits with a load of dangerous drugs. It was an excellent plan; carrying it out was the only problem.)

"That's my watch," Kasper said.

"True. Do you want to take it back?"

He nodded. I unclasped the Rolex and held it out to Kasper. He took a step back.

"Put it on the table."

"You'd be better off letting me keep it," I said. "If you bothered to read the papers, you'd know that a lot of French cops are corrupt. When they arrest you later, they'll pinch it from you. Leave it with me. I'll hold on to it for when you get out of prison when you're ninety-five."

"You're bluffing."

"I'm not. But you know that. You know you're fucked. I don't even understand why you're still here. If I were you, I'd already have left the country."

"Put your shoes on."

"It's because you're not simply an assassin," I said as I slipped on my left shoe. "You've got investments in this organization. And you've got something in the oven."

"In the oven?"

"Yeah. You've got a batch of heroin baking," I said as I tied my shoe. "And you're stuck here because the conversion reaction has begun. And when the reaction has begun, you've got to follow it through to the end."

"We're almost finished," said Kasper.

"You'd have been better off abandoning your investment and getting out."

"Face the wall."

I faced the wall. I heard Kasper moving, and then he told

me to turn around. I turned around. He'd put his Rolex back on his left wrist.

"Walk in front of me," he ordered, pointing at the door with the barrel of his PPK. "Walk slowly."

I obeyed. We went down a bare, deserted hallway. At the end of the hallway was an iron door with a security bar, and a sleepy young monk sitting on a folding stool. As we drew near, the monk stood up and opened the door, which took him a good two minutes.

"Is the girl downstairs?" I asked Kasper.

He didn't answer. The door opened onto a steep stairway that led down two or three meters. The cinder floor of the cellar was visible. A lightbulb in a cage faintly lit the space.

"Go down, slowly."

I went down, slowly, with Kasper behind me. Above us, the monk closed the heavy door.

At the bottom of the steps I glanced around. The cellar was vast and the caged lightbulbs dirty and few. There were low walls and pillars running or rising here and there, and you could make out the contours of coal piles and reflections on bottles, but on the whole, everything was more or less a dark jumble.

"Go in."

I went in. The soles of our shoes crunched on the cinders.

"Are you going to whack me?"

"Not at the moment."

"Tarpon?" someone called from behind one of the walls.

"Charlotte," I answered.

I went around the wall. Charlotte was sitting on the floor under a yellowish light. One of her arms was half raised; her wrist was handcuffed to a pipe. I saw she wasn't injured. So

I relaxed, and my legs began to tremble so uncontrollably that I had to lean against the wall.

"What are you doing? Move it!" said Kasper.

"You okay?" asked Charlotte.

"Yeah. Fine. Fine."

"Turn around."

"I was worried about you," I said to Charlotte.

"Turn around."

"Yeah, yeah. Coming."

I turned around. To my surprise, Kasper struck me in the sternum with the barrel of the PPK and devilish precision. I lost my breath and fell to the floor in excruciating pain, my cheek on the cinder floor. Kasper stuffed his automatic into his pocket. (He was wearing a thick waterproof rain jacket, the sort you wear to go duck hunting, khaki-colored.) He took out handcuffs and a key. I tried to roll myself in a ball, tensing all my muscles to plow into him, but I was completely numb and I only managed to drool on my chin. He cuffed one of my feet to the pipe above a hose fastening, fifty centimeters above the floor. Unsurprisingly, I looked ridiculous with my foot in the air and was reduced to complete uselessness. In addition, Charlotte and I were separated by a good meter.

"Bastard, obscene brute," Charlotte said.

"You ain't seen nothin' yet, my dearest," said Kasper as he got up and walked off in the half-light.

"You should never trust me," I said, practically dislocating my neck in order to look in Charlotte's direction.

"What are you going on about? Did he bop you on the head?"

"In any case," I said, "I did a very dangerous thing bringing you here. But I couldn't have got in without you, because it had to be a couple. And I wanted to get in, because I wanted to defeat them myself. Original sin, as my poor mother says. Do you understand what I'm saying?"

"No."

"But I do. I know what I'm saying."

I began to be able to move my body again. Just then Kasper reappeared, coming from the back of the cellar. He was accompanied by a different young monk with very widely spaced eyes and an especially imbecilic look who was carrying something under his right arm and a sledgehammer in his hand.

"I thought about killing you and burying you somewhere," Kasper said while I was doing all sorts of contortions to try to sit up straight. "It really would make no difference to me. Nonetheless, I'm against killing someone for nothing. In every sense of 'for nothing.' When we've finished our work here, and unhooked you, I think I'll just leave you down here. I don't for a second believe your ludicrous story about the police waiting for us outside. In the end someone will come and find you." (He smiled again.) "At least that's to be hoped."

I managed to rise up on one elbow. The young monk dropped what he was carrying near me. It was a big cobblestone. Without warning, Kasper kicked me in the chest.

Once again, he'd landed on my sternum with atrocious precision. And again I immediately found myself with my cheek in the cinders, eyes half closed, and the get-up-and-go of a washcloth. Kasper took me by the wrist.

"The master is great," said the imbecile young monk without addressing anyone in particular. "The master is good!"

"Before, however," said Kasper, "I owe you something."

He placed my arm on the cobblestone. He took the hammer from the imbecile monk and whacked me on the arm with all his might. Even though he was using his left hand, he broke my arm on the first try.

I experienced a brief moment of shock, lack of feeling, and, especially, disbelief. Kasper placed my other arm on the cobblestone. Then I began to scream my lungs out and yanked away my good arm as best I could. The little monk burst out laughing, grabbed my wrist with both of his hands, put my arm back on the cobblestone, and Kasper brought down his hammer. My second arm broke and so did the hammer's handle.

After that, I don't recall everything. My mind remained locked up in my body but it had a huge desire to escape, and it ran and galloped around my head and tried frantically to break its walls. I know that I screamed enough to destroy my vocal cords. I know that I bit my lower lip so hard that I sliced off a piece of it so that blood was dribbling from it. None of this is charming or heroic. And I know that Charlotte attempted to attack Kasper and that she pulled on her chain like a dog, and she was as enraged as a dog. The little monk was doubled up with laughter. Kasper seemed distant and somewhat disappointed.

I also know that after a short while a man emerged from the shadows at the back of the cellar. Far behind him you could make out a slit of brilliant light coming through the crack in the open door from which he'd entered. He was over sixty and balding. He had large shifty eyes and a bit of whitish hair on the sides and back of his head that hung down his neck in uneven strands. His nose was short and stubby, and he had little rabbit teeth stained with tartar and nicotine, almost uniformly brown. He was pale and his skin was greasy with sweat. He was dressed in a white coarse-linen suit covered in brown and blackish stains and he was wearing rubber gloves like housewives use to do the dishes. A gas mask hung from his fat neck.

"Hey, you, stupid ass!" he said to Kasper with a bewildered yet stern air. "What's going on here? What did you do? What's wrong with that man?"

The bald guy had a Germanic accent. A sharp odor was filling the cellar, no doubt coming from the open door in the back.

"This man is that idiot Tarpon," said Kasper. "I broke both his arms. It'd be best if you went back to your job."

The bald guy shook his head impatiently and stated that the screaming was bothering him. I don't remember how he put it exactly; I was feeling pretty low. I know he went away, and that after a moment he came back and shoved a needle into my arm.

"Murderer! Murderer!" cried Charlotte from somewhere beyond my field of vision, and I vaguely thought that the bald guy was about to do me in, and my mind, oddly, somehow rebelled against this notion; I tried to struggle.

"Relax, officer," said the bald guy. "This will ease your pain."

He was dirty but his gaze was gentle and kindly. I think he smiled at me while he pushed the plunger of the syringe. I felt an unbearable tickling in my palm and a soothing warmth in my upper arm and heart. I thought I was dying. The bald guy had formed a little round pout with his fleshy lips and was whistling, in fact, the *Danse macabre*.

"Hurry up, will you," said Kasper.

"You don't need to stay here."

"I want you to go back to work. I don't want you hanging around."

"It's not good," said the imbecile monk, "it's not good to

tell the master what to do. The master knows. The master is good. Enough nonsense, you! You already broke the hammer!"

"For God's sake, I don't believe it!" grumbled Kasper shaking his head. He left my field of vision and I heard him repeat that he was leaving but he'd be back. And then I lost consciousness for real.

18

WHILE my mind was wandering around in restful empti-
ness, two fascinating things happened.

First, I hadn't managed to fool Kasper, and I hadn't expected to, really, but I'd made him worried. After he walked
out of the cellar where the bald chemist had injected me
with whatever it was, Kasper left the community grounds.
Leaving the 504 behind parked in a shed, he went on foot
to the village center. He entered the snack bar where he
bought a carton of Camels. Then he headed back toward the
institute. On his way, both going and coming, he carefully
and rather discreetly examined the surroundings. He didn't
see anything unusual and so he was reassured.

Meanwhile, peacefully seated under some trees on a hillside, Coccioli and Haymann, a six-pack next to them, were
observing Kasper through binoculars. And they were alarmed
to see that he was still in Doutremait and hadn't gone back
to Paris or fled somewhere else. They also could see that he
was doing some reconnaissance work of his own. Later,
Haymann even told me that they'd thought of intervening
then and there, without waiting for Chauffard, Grazzelloni,
and the others to arrive.

The second really interesting thing that happened while
my mind was wandering all over the place was that Charlotte
went to town on the imbecile monk.

I was on the floor, foot in the air, mouth drooling, chin bloody, and the little monk was also on the floor, sitting on his heels, and he was explaining to Charlotte that the master was good, the master was great. Meanwhile, the master had returned to his den. The slit of light at the back of the cellar had disappeared. The sharp odor of chemicals had begun to subside. Charlotte was crying softly, partly for real and partly to make herself seem like a poor little fragile creature. And then she started to say that she wanted to learn the master's teachings too.

"Well," said the imbecile monk, "it's a bit complicated."

"I want to learn, I want to learn," cried Charlotte. "Look where my miserable life has led me. I've fallen as low as I possibly can. It's the perfect time for me to receive the master's teaching. Can't you see that the shortest road to the summit passes through the base?"

"You speak like the master," said the imbecile monk, looking slightly lost.

"Teach me his word!"

"I'll try," declared the monk after some reflection.

"No!" cried Charlotte. "Give me some water. I cannot listen to you in this impure state. Pour some water on my head!"

"Of course," said the imbecile monk.

He rose, disappeared, and came back a short while later with a pail of water. Charlotte bowed her head with humility. The monk approached her to empty the pail over her head. Don't forget that Charlotte is a professional stunt woman. She drew her feet under her. When the monk bent over, Charlotte quickly leaned forward and slammed his chin with her head. She's a hardheaded woman. She knocked the monk out cold.

Then she reached for the cobblestone and broken hammer. It took her some time because she didn't want to strike so hard as to attract attention, but at last she broke the chain of her handcuffs and freed herself. She looked me over. I didn't look good. She tore the imbecile monk's robe in strips and bound and gagged the zealot using sailor's-knots. Then she picked up the cobblestone and the hammer head and broke the chain on the cuffs holding my foot to the pipe.

Meanwhile—but we knew nothing about this—Kasper had left the grounds but was on his way back. He seemed to be taking his time.

I tried to compose myself and laughed. My impressions were all over the place. I was abulic. My tongue was as saturable as a dirty dishcloth and my forehead was sudating. My perceptions were in tatters and I felt like I was bathing in galipot. I was terribly labile and when Charlotte made me stand up it wasn't breathtaking or amatory, so I spouted curse words and even insulted her, staggering like an Ophite. Well, you get the picture. And on top of it, I was high as a goat.

Charlotte—who could not exactly grab me by my broken arms—pushed and pulled me toward the stairway, cursing under her breath like a teamster. When we got to the stairs, I tripped and fell and let out a roar because I was in pain. I stood up and walked ahead in the dim light, groaning, head down. I trampled the cinders and bumped into bottles, empty crates, and coal. Charlotte stumbled behind me.

"Not that way," she said. "Can you understand what I'm saying? Oh, fudge, Tarpon, what did they do to you?"

She seemed mad with concern about my poor little self, and her concern made me ecstatic, but I didn't have the presence of mind to answer her. I even bumped into her and almost ran into a door in the middle of the wall that seemed to block off an entire rear portion of the cellar. Getting out of the cellar was a good idea. I started kicking at the door.

"Stop that! Stop!" (Charlotte stepped between me and the door and winced when I kicked her in the shin by mistake.)

"It's locked from your side, you poor slob," remarked a drunken voice that I recognized.

"Well, well," I said to Charlotte. "If it isn't Renée Mouzon."

Charlotte looked at me. She turned toward the door. She grabbed the key in the lock and opened it.

"No one move," she said.

No one moved. No one was in a state to be able to.

Through the doorway, we could see a double living room, with three steps separating a first level from a second. There were no windows and the walls were white, not whitewashed like everywhere else in the institute but painted in matte white. To the right of the door stood a chair, a small Louis XVI writing desk, and a large lamp with a shade, held up by a naked Black woman made of heavy metal painted red, gold, and black. That lamp was lit, and there were several fluorescent tubes on the ceiling that were lit as well, and similar tubes in other parts of the space beyond the three steps, and additional torchères there. Together they projected bright light onto the display case to the left of the door, on portraits of Hitler and Freud in the other room, and, at the back of this room, on a huge bed across from the door. In the display case were jewels and weapons. There were rings, bracelets, necklaces, and tiaras. There were horse pistols, dueling pistols, a halberd, a samurai sword in its sheath, a Spanish-looking breastplate adorned with gold arabesques. Across from the door on the bed sat Renée Mouzon and Philippine Pigot.

Philippine Pigot looked like her pictures. She was sitting at the head of the bed with her back against the wall and her legs straight out in front of her, turning toward us the soles of her shoes, her torso, and her dead eyes. She was smiling exhaustedly. At the other end of the bed, Renée Mouzon was trying to prop herself up on one elbow. Mascara ran down her cheeks and her hair was disheveled. There was a carafe on the floor within her reach, half-full of a topaz liquid. A cigarette hung from her lipstick-smeared mouth. She winked at me flirtatiously.

"Hello there, country boy," she said.

"Hi," I grumbled.

I was coming back to earth. It was hard; I had to make a conscious effort. For a reason that escapes me now, I found the situation hilarious.

"What's going on in this insane asylum?" Charlotte asked.

"Whoa there, sweetie," said Renée Mouzon.

Her mouth stayed open. Her cigarette fell from her lip and began to burn a hole in the flap of her white bathrobe. Both women wore identical white bathrobes. I walked toward them to pick up the cigarette, but I couldn't because my arms were broken.

"Philippine," I said. "Philippine? Hey!"

"She can't hear you, country boy. Her papa is drugging her."

"He's not her papa."

"Papa. Papa," Philippine said.

"I'm here," said the bald guy.

He came in right behind me, his gas mask still hanging around his neck. Charlotte and I turned toward him, somewhat shook up. He didn't seem threatening. He closed the door behind him. He held the key in his hand. He put it in the keyhole on the inside but did not lock the door.

"Papa, Papa, Papa," repeated Philippine, smiling and nodding. Saliva was bubbling at the corners of her lips.

"He's not your papa," I said. "His name is Bachhauffer."

Philippine shook her head from left to right. She kept right on shaking it faster and harder until her hair became disheveled too. She stopped smiling. She pursed her lips. Her expression grew sullen and shifty. I turned around to face Bachhauffer who was leaning against the door. He looked at me calmly and innocently.

"I'm wondering if you're not batty," I said. "At least somewhat."

I giggled. I don't know what Charlotte was doing just then. I imagine she was trying to think and lie low. In any case, I'm sorry she had to go through that, seeing as she was the only one of us functioning normally in a room where Philippine and I were doped up, Renée Mouzon was drunk, and Bachhauffer was completely away with the fairies.

"You're German," I said. "You're a Nazi bastard. Perhaps you've forgotten with time. No, you haven't forgotten!" (I tried to point to the portrait of Hitler across the room, but I only managed to wave my broken right arm grotesquely. I cried out in pain.) "I don't know!" I shouted. "You worked with the French gestapo, or in any case you worked with Fanch Tanguy for a long time because you whistle just like he did, you whistle like Fanch the Whistler."

"Papa?" mumbled Philippine, trying to concentrate.

"You were with him when he was murdered by those Basques. I don't know what happened to you after. I don't know what you've been doing since 1944, but—"

"I was in Argentina."

"Ah," I said, catching my breath. "So. In other words, you understand what I'm saying. You were in Argentina. You really should have stayed there."

"I had to spread my teachings."

I stared at him. "Ah. You really believe that."

For a moment he looked completely confused, then ashamed. He lowered his eyes to the floor, like a child who's been caught out.

"Of course not," he said lightly. "It's just a gimmick. A bunch of hokum. Forgive me, I'm a bit tired."

"You've got a good cover," I stated. "It's quite a difficult way of organizing things, but I suppose your phony sect and all those idiots' spa vacations must turn a tidy profit, in addition to the drug trafficking."

"Shhh!" said Bachhauffer. "Don't mention that. Yes, I have a lot of money."

"How amusing," I said. "You have a lot of money and you stay shut up in that cellar." (I raised my chin abruptly.) "Well, you go out on occasion."

"Of course."

"Of course," I repeated. "And you ran into Philippine. I was thinking that she ran into you when she disappeared, and you brought her here. But that's not it. You went to the Baudrillart Foundation, I don't know when, but it was a long time ago. She was still working there, and she heard you whistle. That shook her up. She must have mentioned it to her mother, let something slip. And that's why, when she disappeared, Marthe Pigot brought up Fanch Tanguy—"

"Papa! Papa!" Philippine exclaimed enthusiastically from the back of the room.

"I don't know," said Bachhauffer, sounding bored.

Here in the cellar, and outside too, it was 5:40 p.m. I didn't know it because I had lost all notion of time as well as a number of other notions. Nor did I know that Chauffard and Grazzelloni had arrived early, at 5:30, with eleven other cops, in four cars. I didn't know they were fanning out around the farm.

I hadn't fooled Kasper, but I'd worried him. He'd returned to the farm after his little reconnaissance mission in the village. He was somewhere upstairs, worried and impatient. He was surveying the surrounding countryside. And something attracted his eye, a stealthy movement in the bushes, or maybe the sun reflected on some binoculars . . . something. So he examined the environs more attentively, and he must have noticed that there were people surrounding the Community of Reformed Skoptsy. He calculated the risks and figured he had the time to take the money with him.

Meanwhile, back in the cellar, Bachhauffer and I were chatting amiably.

"Why on earth did you drug that child?" I was asking as I laughed stupidly.

"I was a little confused and disoriented," said Bachhauffer. "They brought her here, locked her up in my quarters, and she called me Papa. They wanted to kill her, you know!"

"Daddy!" shouted the drugged girl from the back of the room, just to change things up.

"I don't want them to kill her, I don't want anyone to die at all!" exclaimed Bachhauffer forcefully. "It's not necessary, she's a half-wit. I made them understand. They just have to stay calm. She simply needs to be drugged. They listened to me because I'm a great chemist. How odd! After all these years, the daughter of my good comrade Fanch Tanguy—"

The door opened behind Bachhauffer. It hit him in the back, shoving him off to one side. Kasper came in energetically, PPK in hand. He stood still for a brief moment when he saw me and our eyes met, but I could read in his that he had much bigger fish to fry. He moved to the side, crossed the room, and with a single stride climbed over the three steps and walked toward Hitler's portrait.

"Well, well, where are your manners?" protested Bachhauffer, rubbing his elbow and taking a few small steps as if to follow Kasper.

I made a slight movement toward the open door. Bachhauffer glanced at me and leapt with startling clairvoyance and nastiness between me and the door. He slammed it closed and turned the key in the lock.

"Oh, no you don't! You're staying here! Everyone stays locked up in here!"

Meanwhile, Kasper had grabbed the portrait of Adolf off the wall and sent it flying into the middle of the room. Behind the portrait was a large Fichet wall safe. Kasper placed one knee on the ground and his PPK next to it. In a flash, he opened the safe. Charlotte set off like an arrow toward him. Kasper picked up his automatic and didn't even need to aim it at Charlotte; she stopped dead in her tracks two meters from him and I started breathing again.

"Okay," said Charlotte, putting her hands in the air. "Don't be angry with me. I just wanted to try..." (She walked slowly backwards.)

"Go to the back of the room and face the wall," said Kasper.

"Do what he says," I told Charlotte.

She obeyed. Bachhauffer, looking confused, was walking toward Kasper, but very slowly, one step at a time, with a meditative pause between each step. Philippine Pigot had sat up on the edge of the bed, knees bent, hands flat on either side of her. She craned her neck, lifted her chin, and listened attentively. Her nostrils flared; she seemed to be sniffing the air around her. As for Renée Mouzon, she was crashed out, snoring.

"What are you doing?" Bachhauffer asked.

Kasper didn't answer. Again he placed his PPK on the ground, pulled a large plastic bag out of the safe, and grabbed it with his teeth. He snatched his automatic and stood up. The bag was heavy. You could see the muscles of his jaw tremble with effort as his top lip turned upward. In the distance, I heard a soft, sharp click and it took me two or three seconds to realize it was the sound of a gunshot.

"Where are you taking my money?" asked Bachhauffer.

"Open the door."

I noticed that Bachhauffer had the key in his hand. Kasper aimed the PPK at his stomach.

"You have no right to take my money," said Bachhauffer.

"Daddy's dough," said Philippine dreamily, but no one was paying her the slightest attention and Kasper started to shout: "It's my money! It's the organization's money! We let you play with it, that's all, you shitty little chemist."

I don't know if he was hoping to give Bachhauffer a salutary shock with his foul language, or if he was simply losing control. Whatever it may be, the chemist let out a sort of squeal then threw himself at Kasper, yammering in German things beyond my understanding.

Kasper fired. I saw the projectile exit under Bachhauffer's shoulder blade; it made a hole in his work clothes. He shrieked, and so did Philippine. Then, using his momentum, the chemist slammed into Kasper, who shot another bullet into him at close range. Bachhauffer fell screaming and grabbing at the plastic bag. The bag tore. A big strip of plastic remained in Kasper's teeth as dozens and dozens of five-hundred-franc bills scattered around in clumps, like chewed artichoke leaves.

Charlotte unstuck herself from the wall with the obvious intention of jumping on Kasper's head. I stuck out my leg and the darling girl tripped and fell flat on the floor.

"Stay calm, for God's sake!" I ordered. "I love you!"

On all fours, Charlotte looked up at me open-mouthed, completely stunned. Meanwhile, Kasper was aiming his gun at us, shouting.

"Pick up my money!" he cried. "Pick up my money! Put it in my pockets."

"Drop dead," I said.

He let himself fall to the ground. I thought he was having some sort of breakdown, but it was simply to place his arm in its cast on the floor so that his fingertips could touch the key near Bachhauffer's corpse. His fingers were numb, but he managed to grab the key after two or three tries, and he stood back up.

In the meantime, Philippine Pigot had moved without anyone noticing her. She was now lying on Bachhauffer's corpse and palpating it. She brought her bloodstained fingers toward her face and tasted the liquid with the tip of her tongue.

"Don't try to stop me," Kasper said to us.

He was calmer. He'd understood that he wouldn't be taking the money with him. He walked toward the door.

"My papa," said Philippine Pigot. "You hurt my papa."

She swept her arm through the air and managed to hook Kasper's ankle. He did a sort of entrechat and stumbled. Now the blind girl was grasping his foot. Kasper smacked her on the head with the barrel of the PPK and she cried out in pain, letting go. Kasper rushed to the door.

Muffled by the thickness of the walls and foundations, the sounds of a veritable gun battle now resounded somewhere on the farm. Kasper managed to stick the key in the lock on the first try, even with his numb fingers. At the same time, with his left arm, he kept the gun aimed at us, in such a way that Charlotte remained calm. And me, armless as I was, I didn't see what I could possibly do.

Turning the key, on the other hand, was not so easy for Kasper. It took him an entire minute. And meanwhile, Philippine Pigot had stood up, her face twisted in a terrible rage. A trickle of blood flowed from her skull into her eye. She walked across the room, bumping into the walls until she reached the display case with the weapons. She broke the glass pane with both fists at once, and the glass cut her wrists, and more blood flowed. Then, before Kasper could see her, and before Charlotte could do anything, the blind girl pulled the large Japanese sword from its sheath and, guided by the noise Kasper was making with his key, headed straight into him, raising her arms bathed in scarlet and striking him on the head with the big tarnished blade.

I think Kasper was already dead, his head split open like a radish, when his finger pressed the trigger one last time. He had just managed to unlock the damn door. And Commissioner Chauffard, with his scruffy mustache and his Terrier, opened the door at that precise moment and took in everything at a glance: Charlotte on all fours, Renée Mouzon snoring, Bachhauffer dead on the floor, the blind girl who had just fallen with a bullet in her lung, and me like a sap, and then Kasper, who fell on top of Chauffard as his brains emptied out all over his trousers.

19

I'M FINISHING writing at home what I began in the hospital. After Chauffard appeared, it seems I sort of fainted. Maybe from the pain in my arms, maybe from nausea. I vaguely remember the moment I was crossing the courtyard of the farm. I was lying on a stretcher. Near the gate, inside the courtyard, there was a car that had rammed into the wall, and it had burned in part, but now the fire was out. At the back of the courtyard, twenty or thirty little monks and nuns were sitting on the ground in the mud, hands on their heads, guarded by three plainclothes officers whom I didn't know, one of whom was holding a machine gun. Because of their shaved heads and their hands on said heads, the monks and nuns looked like they belonged in a photo of some colonial war.

I was carried through the gate and put in an ambulance where there were gendarmes. Charlotte got in with me. Through the open gate, I could see five or six guys coming out of the offices in single file with their hands on their heads, flanked by Coccioli and Haymann, and two or three other officers with revolvers. Next the bald Buddhist nun appeared. Someone was helping her walk. She seemed to be injured and she was crying. I don't remember seeing any of the clients. Apparently later some of them made claims that they had been brutalized. In any case, the gendarmes closed the ambulance doors and I passed out.

So, as for all the violence, it's over, but I suppose I should still say what happened to the protagonists.

As for the gang, all of its members whom we could get our hands on are now in the slammer, including Lionel Constantini, the guys who had fired on the ring road, and those who were picked up at the institute, including the little dark-haired guy from the house in the forest. Georges Rose, too, and several of his employees from the Baudrillart Foundation, and his employer, Deputy Mauchemps. Most of the little monks and nuns, having managed to prove they were imbeciles, were released and had to reenlist in other sects of one sort or another.

Inquiries are ongoing regarding certain police or other government officials who possibly covered up the actions of criminals, but these inquiries are not moving forward clearly or quickly. As for Chauffard and the others, they were hailed in the press, and the Minister of the Interior and the Minister of Justice exchanged bittersweet words about them during two or three public appearances. In the end, they received neither compensation nor punishment.

Let's not forget Mr. Jude and his cash problems. Three days after the bloody conclusion of this can of worms, he showed up at my place where he found Charlotte tidying. He handed her what he owed me and said I didn't have to bother with his affair any longer.

"But your affair is over," Charlotte said. "Mr. Tarpon knows who was stealing from you."

"So do I," said Jude, "and I'm telling you he doesn't need to concern himself with it anymore."

He seemed very embarrassed and was sweating, according

to Charlotte, and he left after that. Charlotte, who sees evil everywhere, thinks that Jude is the lover of his dishonest assistant, Huguette, and this explains his bizarre behavior. She's probably right.

Nick Malrakis returned to the fold. Charlotte and he had an argument over his jacket, the one Charlotte had loaned me. Nick left in anger. I think they're going to get a divorce.

Jean-Baptiste Haymann put a little extra in his cookie jar by selling a few exclusive articles about the affair, and otherwise went back to his retired life in Clamart. He comes almost every day to play chess or other games with me. He taught me Chinese chess, Japanese chess, and Go. I play all those games very badly. He wins every time and laughs triumphantly.

I came home as soon as I could, because hospitals are expensive. My fractures showed up clearly on the X-rays and they were easy to fix. Soon my casts will come off. My bones will remain fragile where they were broken. It's a shame, but nothing can be done.

I think I'll stay in this profession but will try from now on to not get smacked on the arms and use my head more. I'm still learning English and also reading the sociological novels that Haymann brings me and the extremist political ones that Charlotte brings me. I'm going to keep doing my job even though I don't like it. I told you before that it's no fun to track down deadbeats while drug traffickers are sitting on the National Assembly. That having been said, I seemed to have been hoping for a big job that would finally allow me to do Good on a large scale, like firemen do. Well, I had my big job and got absolutely no satisfaction from it.

Now that I can move about, I went twice to the movies and several times to the examining magistrate. I haven't been convicted of killing Madrier and don't think I ever will be. The concierge brings me my meals on a regular basis. Charlotte comes too, several times a week on average, but has started coming less often lately. Perhaps we'll go to bed together once my casts have been taken off.

But for now, I'm mostly exhausted.

OTHER NEW YORK REVIEW CLASSICS

For a complete list of titles, visit www.nyrb.com.